Mystery and Malice aboard RMS Ballast

The Eighth Anty Boisjoly Mystery

Mystery and Malice aboard RMS Ballast

1. Tales of Sails and Betrayals and for Some Reason Mails..........1

2. The Queasy Affair of the Mal-de-Mer..........11

3. Dare Daring To Do Daring Derring-Do..........21

4. Times as Drastic as Limes in Aspic..........30

5. Not At All A Tall Atoll..........42

6. The Import In Port In Port..........48

7. The Ennobling Victory of Balthazar Tiptree..........60

8. A Splash of Dash, A Lash of Brash, and One Last Flash of Panache..........72

9. Bunny Babbit's Billiards Habits..........81

10. The Power of the Pledge Between Hightower and Hedge..........90

11. Murmurs Made of Murders Made by Mermaids..........102

12. All the World's a Wager, and All the Men and Women Merely Punters..........109

13. Of Snitches and Riches and Infinite Ipswiches..........119

14. The Vices and Vulnerabilities of a Vickers in Vigor..........129

15. The Rime of the Ancient Marinated..........137

16. A Wary Wherry to a Scarey Skerry..........150

17. The View of the Isle from Pilyek Pile..........159

18. Cardall's Clever Cure-All..........169

19. The Measure of Whether the Treasure is Nether..........174

20. The Seamless Scheme of the Scheme Unseen within the Seeming Scheme..........184

21. The Twist Missed in the Mist..........193

Aft..........204

Tales of Sails and Betrayals and for Some Reason Mails

I'd been a passenger aboard the yacht of Archie Lord Hannibal-Pool on many occasions and had never until now had cause to believe he was an outlaw of the high seas.

In my defence, that was before the piracy, buried treasure, mutiny, and murder, and prior to being assigned a starboard stateroom for a westbound voyage. These things add up.

The tally started on one of those crisp, maritime, good-fishing mornings that seem to be sunrise all day long, and indeed this particular morning was a mid-afternoon on the tip of Victoria Pier in Portsmouth, detour and moor of *RMS Ballast,* flagship of Archie Lord Hannibal-Pool's toybox. The air was a brisk mist of tar and salt and hazard. The water hopped and chopped and chivvied even the biggest boats of steam and sail as they crowded and crossed each other in the harbour straight. Spires and stacks and smoke and streamers filled the skyline like city blocks, flying the flags of all nations. On the decks and docks and depots a thousand sailors and stevedores performed ten thousand tasks. And so flowed, inexorably onward, the arteries of maritime commerce.

I typically make a point of joining a crossing at the last minute or, ideally, after departure at some sunny port on the itinerary, because there always seems to be so much to do, otherwise, what with the boarding of essentials like champagne and caviar and what must be countless utilities and utensils essential to keeping the boat on the right side of sea level. Today was exceptional, though, because I was bringing a guest.

"Your Lordship, Inspector Ivor Wittersham, of Scotland Yard," I pomped. "Inspector Wittersham, Lord Hannibal-Pool."

Archie Lord H-P, as a rule, neither insists on nor knows the conventions of noble address, but I knew from one giddy tea at Claridge's that the inspector fairly marvels at them, like a small child or fully-grown Boisjoly watching fireworks.

Nevertheless, Ivor and Archie shook hands and parried pleasantries and if anything both parties appeared to be only barely repressing some unspoken animosity. This was possibly down to Archie presenting, as he tends to do, less as a member of the peerage and more a commoner with boat worries. He was wearing a slick sou'wester and a distracted frown on his scrupulously unshaven face, and a newsagent's cloth cap struggled to contain his tempest of white hair.

Ivor was kitted out for a maritime outing exactly as he dresses for his day-to-day professional activities or anything else, I expect, and I've little doubt that he got married in a pigeon-grey trench coat and slapdash moustache.

Of the three of us only I — or at any rate my valet — appeared to have approached the theme of the day in anything like the right spirit. I was fitted out in fully nautical double-breasted, from a twilled navy yachting suit to a pea jacket, over a streamlined, youthful hull and beneath a masting of chestnut locks. I fancy I looked like a young Admiral Lord Nelson conferring with a couple of swabs.

"*RMS Ballast.*" Ivor slung a sailor's rucksack over his shoulder with a practised ease. "Unusual christening for a yacht, I'd have thought, Your Lordship."

The tide was high and *RMS Ballast* rolled on moody tides fully two decks above us and one below. It was a splendid sloop of steam and sail refitted only eight years earlier in 1921 with the lines and lifts and folds and flourishes of the beginning of its Art Deco era. It looked rather like a fedora that sleeps sixteen.

"It's what the lads on the rowing team at Oxford used to call me," explained Archie. "Ballast. I thought it quite funny to give the name to my yacht, at the time."

"I was referring to the prefix." Ivor nodded at the prow of *The Ballast.* "Is RMS not typically reserved for vessels with a charter from the Royal Mail?"

"Just so." Archie gestured about us at the chevy and stride of the bustling ports and piers and ships and shipping of the centre of international commerce that is the maritime hive of Portsmouth. "I do have a Royal Mail charter. It's how I come to have mooring rights here."

"Of course." Ivor issued Archie and myself a cheeky salute and bounded onto the gangplank. "Thanks very much for having me aboard, Your Lordship. I'm very much looking forward to the voyage."

Archie watched Ivor leap onto the main deck where he was met by what appeared to be either a first mate or a cutthroat assassin — it's very difficult to know without a close-up look at the tattoos.

"You weren't tempted to mention that your guest was a detective inspector, Anty?"

"Utterly bent on the idea," I assured him. "But for some reason he didn't want it put about."

"Happily, Lottie recognised his name from *The Times,"* said Archie, referring to Her Ladyship, Charlotte Hannibal-Pool.

"You have no objection, I take it?"

"No, no real objection, to speak of."

"I mean to say, we're only touring the Isle of Wight — what can you possibly smuggle from the Isle of Wight? Temperate weather?"

"Yes, that'll do, Anty, we'll have no more talk of smuggling, if you can manage," said Archie. "And we're not going to the Isle of Wight. Not straight away, in any case."

"Where are we going?"

"Scilly."

"Surely we can be silly on the Isle of Wight," I contended. "I'm prepared to wager that, if we put our minds to it, we could carry it off right here."

"Not silly, Anty, Scilly. The Scilly Islands."

"Not really," I said. "Have you ever been there?"

"Of course I've been there, Anty. Dozens of times." Archie gazed in a vaguely south-westerly direction, as though to demonstrate that he knew the way to Scilly. "Our Royal Mail charter is the extended Scillies."

"All the more time to get acquainted," I said thinking, explicitly and exclusively, of Frederica Hannibal-Pool, His Lordship's niece.

"With your inspector, you mean?"

"Yes."

"Freddy's on board, too, you know."

"Is she?" I paltered, for I knew the entire passenger list, and Freddy's presence on it was the sole reason that I was on it. "Anyone else I know?"

"Your cousin, Theodora…" Teddy Quillfeather, who told me that Freddy would be on board. "…Caspian Starbuck…" The Honourable Caspar, old navy family and merchant marine money, possible rival for the affections of Freddy. "…Harry Babbit…" Bunny Babbit. Splendid chap, if a little wet and weedy, and woozy for my cousin Teddy. "…Dare Flashburn…" No idea. "…no idea who that is. Then there's Lottie and the crew, of course."

"How is Commodore Bittleswill?" I asked. "Still missing the one eye?"

4

"The commodore is taking a bit of a shore leave, this trip." Archie nodded in time with *The Ballast* as she dipped and rose. "We use another chap when we go to Scilly." *The Ballast* nodded again, somehow knowingly. "We're going to need to cast off shortly, Anty. Are your things on board?"

"Still waiting for my man." I surveyed the dock. "I left him at the station."

His Lordship took his haunted expression up the gangplank, leaving me only the cryptic promise, "I'll send Minty."

And in that instant, a car horn tootled from shore and a smart red convertible coupé with the top down skidded onto the pier. The electric flapper behind the wheel was a bob-tailed Quillfeather, in her natural habitat, and in the passenger seat was Vickers, gentleman's personal gentleman to the last of the Boisjolys.

"What ho, Anty." Teddy stood up in the car. "Look who I found at the station, offering two shillings a dance."

"I was doing nothing of the sort, sir," claimed Vickers. "I was looking for your trunk."

"And to gain the best possible vantage from which to look," added Teddy, "he was standing on your trunk."

"That much is true," admitted Vickers. The Boisjoly gentlemen have valued the valeting of Vickers for at least three generations and recent archaeological findings have indicated that he's no longer a young man. It's a happy confluence of circumstance, then, that his short-term memory, routine, and tea-making has become a scattering smattering of serendipity at just the generation that appreciates it. Otherwise, as a single example to hand, I might never have started the trend among the smart set of attending the opera with a hip flask of hot custard.

Teddy hopped out of the car, a manoeuvre for which she had accordingly dressed in a short shimmy dress of a nautical design with royal blue and white piping and buttons, and a matching navy cap clipped onto her brunette bob. Vickers, in keeping with his position, unfolded from the passenger seat like a garden chair with a tricky spine and formal dress sense.

The scarred assassin appeared again on the gangplank. He was compact in a tightly-wound sort of way, and short and ruddy and raw, like a ham, and he wore a striped sailor's jersey and flare-leg trousers and a knitted red cap. This was, it soon transpired, First Mate Clement 'Minty' Moy and, what with all of the above plus a pronounced Emerald Isle accent, he had evidently sprung whole from the pen of Robert Louis Stevenson. He was accordingly nimble and able and he was boarding our steamer trunks and Vickers in the time it took Teddy to clip down the pier.

"Can't tell you how spiffing it is that you made it, Ants. Couldn't have faced exile at sea without an ally."

"Always glad to be of service, Teddy," I spoke only the truth, "but you could have just demurred, couldn't you?"

"I could not." Hands on hips, Teddy began surveying the lines of the *RMS Ballast*. "I have to give Mama one of these little victories once every season — she won't sleep a full night until I'm married and plotting to offload my own daughter — and this short coastal tack seems manageable. There are three breaded bachelors on board, not counting you — I could KO three comers with one brain tied behind my back."

"Is that what this excursion is in aid of, then, marrying you off?"

"It is." Teddy smiled at her mother's stratagems the way one smiles at a child telling a joke. "The poor pip. Thinks I'm too old to have standards. The only real requirement I place on a chap is that he be in the distant future, after I've run out of new dance steps and cocktails and false names given in jest."

"Perfectly reasonable set of criteria, to my mind."

"This is one of the chief differences between you and my mother," observed Teddy. "It's why I'm glad it's you here and not her, much as I love you both."

"Nothing I wouldn't do for my favourite cousin, Teddy, even unto chaperoning you into the infinite wend, with uncountable weeks and unsoundable deeps betwixt me and London's West End."

This was, in spirit, true. Teddy's one of those gravitational bobbins always at the centre of some novel turpitude about which you want nothing more than to be able to say, 'yes I know — I was there.'

This voyage was, however, the culmination of a complex scheme to win the heart of Freddy Hannibal-Pool, with whom I had been corresponding care of the Ladies' Auto Club, a secret address provided by Teddy. This contingency was made necessary by a coolness that had quite suddenly developed between myself and Freddy's father (and younger brother to Lord Hannibal-Pool). There was no explanation for it but no mistaking it, either. The last time I saw him — I recall because it was during the investiture of Bishop Wilson when Cores Pommeroy and I wore armour to evensong — he asked me to cease paying my addresses to his daughter. Inscrutable, I call it.

"It's one day," said Teddy. "One orbit around the Isle of Wight, with an anchorage at Ventnor to give each contestant two dances and a turn around the deck under moonlight. Mama and I have a verbal contract."

"Lord Archie tells me we're detouring to the Scilly Islands," I said. "To deliver the mail."

"Are the silly islands far?" asked Teddy. "They sound like they enjoy being chased."

"No idea. I've only ever been to the continent on *The Ballast,*" I recalled. "As it happens, the last occasion was for me very much like this one is for you — my mother insisted I join the voyage at Valencia so that I might become acquainted with Lord and Lady Hannibal-Pool's daughter."

"Winnifred," provided Teddy.

"If you like," I allowed. "I could only recall the nickname she earned before we left harbour — 'The Winds of Whinge'."

7

"I thought she was a lovely girl."

"She most absolutely is," I confirmed. "All the bits in just the right place and order and one of those sultry, pouty dials that make Hollywood go round. She's also among that inadequately rare breed of bird who can find happiness only in complaint. The girl's principal form of social interaction is the petty grievance."

"You exaggerate, Anty. It's what I love about you."

"The sky, in her adamant view, was too blue," I reported. "It clashed with her bathing costume which, incidentally, was white."

"Well, I think you're a brave little sailor for coming out today."

"The Winds of Whinge, I'm happy to report, is married, and the seas are once again safe."

"Then why did you bring your own policeman?"

"How does everyone know about that already? Inspector Wittersham asked me to invite him as only 'an acquaintance'. I suggested 'dear friend' but he expressed himself unlikely to be able to carry it off for long."

"Is this in aid of one of your mysterious adventures?"

"Not directly," I said. "I mentioned *The Ballast* as complementary detail of an instructive anecdote, and the inspector asked if I might smuggle him aboard next time it departs from Portsmouth."

"He's not unmarried and wealthy, is he?"

"Most decidedly neither."

"Then he can stay," permitted Teddy. "Shall we board? The sooner I start breaking hearts the sooner they'll heal."

"What about your motorcar?" I reminded her. "You're not just leaving it there."

"My car is in London." Teddy nodded at the red coupé. "That belongs to a chap I met at the train station. He very kindly offered me a lift to the pier — via the scenic route — but then he said there was only room for two. I didn't want to argue the point, so I sent him to tip the porter and Vickers and I borrowed the motor. He'll know where to find it."

We bounded up the gangplank, at the top of which was Captain Ahab.

"Barjelly?" asked the wide, wizened, weathered bellwether in leather-patched pea coat and cloth merchant marine captain's cap. He had a brass telescope and a salty scowl and, rounding out the stereotype to a nicety, a parrot on his shoulder.

"It's pronounced 'Beaujolais', like the wine region," I gently corrected. "Anthony, to my shipmates, or simply Anty, should you need a quick ship-to-shore semaphore."

"Captain Slapton," arr'd the pirate. "And you'd be Miss Quillfeather."

"Teddy, if you like," offered Teddy. "What a pretty parrot."

"Macaw," said the macaw.

"This be Albert Ross," introduced the captain.

"Looks like a parrot," persisted Teddy.

"Macaw," repeated the bird with a touch of pique.

"You're the last to board." Slapton made boarding last sound notoriously unlucky. "We best be casting off at next tick o'clock and clear these shallows while we still can."

Slapton narrowed his gaze at something distinctly untrustworthy somewhere between us and the greyed, frayed horizon.

"Aye, Minty and me best be making sail…"

"Ak!" squawked Albert Ross. "Minty and I."

"Aye," conceded Slapton, "Minty and I best be making sail. I don't much care for the snout of that cloud bank — it be the knife edge of a howler or I'm a landlubbing Londoner." The captain took hold of a liberal portion of my shoulder and pulled me into a louring squint. "There's danger and death awaits us in the Scilly Seas, you mark my words."

Clearly, I did precisely that — one marks those sorts of words rather by default — but I had no idea how prescient they would turn out to be.

CHAPTER TWO

The Queasy Affair of the Mal-de-Mer

RMS Ballast is an opulent great tub of polished oak and brass, sumptuously spread over three decadent decks and sixteen stately staterooms above the water line. There's a drawing room, billiards room, dining room (not to be confused with the al fresco luncheon deck), smoking bar, and library, obviously, and there's a first-class galley of the kind and quality that precipitated the fall of Rome.

The Ballast galley was probably as well-equipped as that of any royal yacht but the kitchen culture derived entirely from the tastes and talents of Chef Syds Carvell and his symphony of dedicated specialists, including a chap who'd been educated from adolescence in the theory and practice of basting. The skills of the team, superlative as they were, were nevertheless surpassed to a standstill by Chef Syds' unshakeable insistence on the very best of everything — beluga caviar from only happily married sturgeons, champagne from the first press of hand-peeled grapes, Iberian hams so aged they had to be acquired at estate sales. I hastened to my cabin to dress for dinner.

Happily, I had reviewed Vickers' packing before setting out for the train and had replaced my golfing plus-fours with a white dinner jacket, and hence was a very tidy sight indeed when I quit my cabin moments later only to find myself face-to-face with the grim pallor of green death.

"What ho, Inspector. You're not dressed for dinner. Or much of anything else, if I'm to be entirely candid. Do you mean to be that colour?"

Ivor's stateroom was directly across from mine. He clung to the door frame in topsy-turvy travel tweeds and a face the colour of young cucumber.

"Dinner?" he said as though from the bottom of a pit.

"In the absence of a more grandiose word, yes," I confirmed. "But I can promise you something that describes more as a concerto of cuisine. Last time I was on board the high point of the journey and, I don't think it's understating it, the year, was a bouillabaisse of mussels, prawns, cockles, langoustine, bream, and red mullet merged into a fresh tomato reduction with garlic and oregano, served with anchovy bruschetta and aïoli... Are you quite well, Inspector?"

As I had described the daily specials, Ivor had been groaning from, I assumed, anticipation. But he had also progressively shrunk, bending at the knees and belt-line, and relying more heavily on the door for support.

"Have we left port?"

"Several minutes ago, yes," I reported.

"What? Why?"

"Preliminary to getting where we're going," I explained. "You're not a naval man, so it's understandable you might not know that."

"Is Hannibal-Pool really meaning to take us to the Isles of Scilly?" croaked Ivor.

"He is. How the devil did you know about the detour?"

"Not detour... mail... charter."

"Once again, bang on," I applauded. "Yes, apparently there's mail wants delivering to some Scilly island and His Lordship has elected to put it through instanter. No idea why."

"Because I'm on board." Ivor managed to look in my general direction but sometimes you can just tell when a chap isn't focusing. "His Lordship is a swindler. Has a charter from His Majesty's Post, collects the pay and perks, but there's never any mail."

"You don't mean to say, Inspector, that you took advantage of my friendship to effect an arrest of a member of not only the House of Lords but the Juniper Gentlemen's Club?"

As I spoke, Ivor retreated into his cabin. I followed.

"Just so, Boisjoly — I had no intention of making an arrest. I was bluffing." Ivor lay partially on his bed with both feet on the floor in a position that appeared both acrobatic and maimed. "I assumed that when he realised he'd been rumbled he'd quietly give up the charter. Didn't think he'd actually put to sea with me on board, least of all try to fulfil the terms of the charter."

"Then you should have asked me, Inspector," I gently reprimanded. "I could have told you that if there's one thing that Archie Lord Hannibal-Pool likes more than his yacht, it's the spondoolics which keep it afloat. So this is why you didn't want me to tell anyone that you were the rozzers."

"Exactly. I was counting on the element of surprise."

"Then you should have followed my example and provided a false name," I hindsighted. "Lady Hannibal-Pool recognised yours from the papers. His Lordship was fully prepared with a Scilly Islands pilot and itinerary. There's even a parrot."

Ivor moaned and shifted position, found the new one wanting, tried lifting his legs to the bed, thought the better of it, and slid to the floor where he lay, curled up. He looked unwell and in want of bucking up.

"What you want, Inspector, is a square meal," I advised. "Chef Syds does a seafood gratin that's mostly tentacles under a generous, gummy crust of parmigiano and the ripest gorgonzola... did you speak?"

"No, but if I did I'd say belt up," groaned Ivor. "Stop talking about food. Stop talking. Stop swaying."

"Have you a touch of mal-de-mer, Inspector?"

"Nnnggngngnnn."

"I see," I tweaked. "But I thought you were a sport fisherman."

13

"Placid lakes. Docks. Not raging seas." Ivor pulled himself into a reading chair which he occupied like a bag of jam. "What was the captain thinking, putting to sea in this weather?"

"The waters are actually comparatively calm," I reported. "However the captain did say that he saw a tempest in our direct path."

While Ivor churned this news I dampened a cloth from his water pitcher. He applied it to his forehead and I closed the curtains over all his cabin portholes.

"You need dark and calm." I spoke in sanitorium tones. "I shall sit with you, and sing you soft songs of caprice and fancy. Do you know any songs of caprice and fancy?"

"What you can do for me, Mister Boisjoly, is get Hannibal-Pool to turn this boat around and take me back to civilised ground."

"That may indeed be a more productive use of my talents," I agreed. "Right oh, Inspector, you stay here and try not to think of the oscillating waves and lurching horizon, I'll see if I can't at least get you put ashore at the nearest uncharted island paradise."

I am a good friend if the standard is that, had he insisted, I'd have remained at Ivor's bedside. If, however, I'd be expected to do so happily I'd fall leagues short of the mark. If I'm honest, I was quite looking forward to sharing fizzy preprandials with my fellow passengers in anticipation of whatever divinity Chef Syds and his flight of angels had stewed up.

The drawing room of *RMS Ballast* is done up like an American bar. The walls are brass piping over rosewood in geometric relief for an effect not unlike having drinks in Coco Chanel's jewellery box. The furniture and fittings and bar counter are all similarly deco, as were the bright young things who greeted me from the port side, sat around a glass and pewter table that looked like the wing of an aeroplane.

"What ho, Ants," hailed Teddy. She sat between and hung her arms over the shoulders of Bunny Babbit and Caspar Starbuck. "Come and make introductions. You know how timid I am."

Archie Lord Hannibal-Pool was tending bar alone and so I made that my first port of call.

"Quick shandy, Anty?" offered Lord Archie.

"You know I've never learned to fully appreciate these pragmatic preserves from the era of tall ships," I admitted. "Just a whisker and water, if you got 'er."

"I don't, actually." Archie assumed a grave countenance. "No whisky at all."

"Blimey, no whisky? For the entire voyage?" I endured the revelation like an Englishman. "Just champagne then, I suppose."

"No champagne either, Anty. Minty managed the liquor stores and he overlooked some basics."

"What have you got?"

"Shandy."

"Just shandy?"

"And grog."

"Right oh. Grog it is, then." I watched his lordship ladle a tankard out of an immense water barrel and I added, with casual disinterest, "Freddy not joining us?"

"Not yet. When I told her you were on board she took to her cabin to review her wardrobe." Archie handed over my sailor's ration of rum and water and followed it into a zone of confidence. "Wants to make an impression, I think."

"Rather wasted on me, I expect." The last time I saw Freddy was at the bar of the Criterion. She was in a pink sequined sack dress with spaghetti straps and a matching fascinator into which she'd gathered her mane of whisky-coloured locks, and she wore reflective rose lipstick and drank a pink gin fizz and she winked at me behind

15

her mother's back. "Can't recall the last time I saw her. Epsom, maybe?"

Caspar Starbuck makes everything he wears look like an admiral's uniform. Today it was a simple double-breasted evening suit and black tie, but over his broad beam and beneath his trim tip and docked beard, it gave the illusion of gravitas, as though bearing the weight of embroidered epaulettes and history. The overall effect was completed with one of those stern scowls that Nelson doubtless had on his face in the days leading up to Trafalgar.

Bunny Babbit, conversely, makes everything he wears look like a sailor suit. There's something fundamentally boyish about the chap, from his fair hair and sleek cheeks to his blue blazer and white breeches and black buckle boots. I know him to be roughly my age but it's a strain to resist giving him a tip and advising him against strong drink.

He was drinking, though. Seemed quite enthusiastic about the practice, in point of fact, and approached it with the air of a man with something to prove.

"Not drinking, Caspar?" I noted that he had no tankard of his own, while Bunny had two. "If it's grog that's putting you off, I'm confident that my man packed an emergency reserve of Glen Glennegie."

"Welcome aboard, Boisjoly," intoned Caspar like a man in mourning. "No, thanks very much. I like to stay alert at the outset of a crossing. You never know when all hands might need to step up."

"Quite so," agreed Bunny theatrically. "Doubtless the captain will be along any minute to get an expert's opinion on South, or to draw on your months of experience to help navigate the tricky passage between the Isle of Wight and England."

"You'll want to watch your intake of gripe water, Bunny," cautioned Caspar. "Doesn't Nursie normally restrict you to one teaspoon before bed?"

Caspar and Bunny, it's worth noting here, are actually quite matey when gambolling together through London's groves and grassy meadows, and as recently as last boat race night, when Caspar was pinched over a small misunderstanding involving an attempt to sail a raft of champagne bottles across Trafalgar Square fountain, it was Bunny who tried to bail him out. What's more, when he realised that he'd loaned his wallet to a barmaid, Bunny offered to take Caspar's place in Bow Street Nick, a ploy which only half worked.

Here on the open sea, however, it's every man for himself in the savage, take-no-prisoners game of impressing Theodora Quillfeather in the time allotted.

In addition to that marble monument physique to which some women respond, Caspian Starbuck is heir to the Earldom of Bustleport and Leep, and his family have been sailors since the invention of water. And, since the investiture of the first Earl of Bustleport and Leep, they usually graduate directly from Dartmouth to the Admiralty. Any Teddy who liked that sort of thing could easily leverage Caspar's now and future social standing into regular tea at the palace and all the grog she could drink.

Henry 'Bunny' Babbit, on the other hand, is none of those things in trump suits. He's built more for speed and manoeuvrability, and he's just the man you want on hand when outrunning a fox. Lightweight and practical for easy shipping. Read history or something at Oxford and has fewer bankable skills than I have, but he does have a pot of money provided by his widowed mother who subsequently married a chap with a diamond mine about six weeks before he fell into it, raising Bunny from a solid and certain future as a vendor of quality pencils to a Mayfair idler and clubman at Boodle's, nominated by no less illustrious a member than Caspian Starbuck.

"Ah, good evening, Your Lordship." This compelling, commanding call came from the night-shaded doorway in which stood the chap who gives handsome lessons to Ronald Coleman. Like the leading man, he had a perfect pencil moustache and sly,

17

knowing grin that lifted at one side, crinkling and twinkling his right eye. He had dark curls at once playful and precise and his dinner jacket had somehow been freshly pressed.

"Evening, Flashburn," replied Archie. "Grog?"

"Love some," projected the Flashburn presence. He collected his tankard and glided to our table, his gaze locked on Teddy's wide, admiring eyes. "You can be none other than Theodora Quillfeather, the most beautiful woman on land or sea."

"Tish," issued Caspar.

"Yish," gagged Bunny.

Flashburn kissed Teddy's hand and finally deigned to notice the rest of us.

"Dare Flashburn."

"Of course you are," said Bunny.

"What ho, Dare." I shook the offered hand. "May I present the Honourable Caspian Starbuck, the slightly less honourable Henry Babbit, and the wholly debauched Anthony Boisjoly — or skipping to the inevitable chumminess ahead, Caspar, Bunny, and Anty."

"Delighted, gentlemen."

"What sort of name is Dare?" asked Bunny.

"It's Daragh, originally," explained Dare, "but people will give one nicknames that reflect one's personality, Bunny, is it?"

"What brings you aboard, Dare?" It was Caspar who asked this but I was wondering the same thing. The other two eligible bachelors on board presented no obstacle nor distraction to my Freddy-centric strategy, but this late dark horse entry risked skewing the odds against the favourite.

"I have business on the Isles of Scilly," replied Dare. "I have many friends in Portsmouth — I have many friends everywhere I've been — and I soon learned that *RMS Ballast* was the next vessel heading my way. His Lordship was kind enough to offer me berth."

"The Isles of Scilly…" I recalled something quite urgent about our destination and, as it happened, in that moment Captain Slapton pushed through the door and pulled it shut behind him.

"A double dip of grog for an old sailor, Your Lordship," called Slapton. "If any of us will be in want of heating fuel tonight, t'is I."

"T'is me," said Albert Ross from the captain's shoulder.

"Aye," agreed Slapton. "T'is me."

"I say, Captain." I joined him at the bar. "If it wouldn't be a tremendous nuisance, could we turn around and go briefly back to port?"

"Eh?" Slapton drew lengthily from his tankard, slammed it down on the bar, issued a theatrical "Aaahh!" and said, "Why would you want to go back to port?"

"In point of fact, I don't. But my guest has slight mal-de-mer, and by 'slight' I mean charybdisian. He's in his cabin, curled tightly into a ball, cursing our seafaring ancestors."

"Wittersham is seasick?" savoured Archie. "Ha! Excellent. We're not turning back."

"We can't turn back," added Slapton. "We're into the slipstream, now. We try to leave it before Scilly there's no telling where we'll end up. You get caught in the channel currents, you run very serious risk of finding yourself dashed on the rocks off Gris Nez, or worse — forced to moor overnight in Belgium."

"My business in Scilly is quite urgent, Anty," said Dare. "I'm sure your friend will gain his sea legs soon enough."

"I hope not," added Archie.

"What is your Scilly business, then, Dare?" asked Bunny.

"Just a lark, really." Dare waved larkly. "I'm after pirate treasure."

"You and thousands of others," commented Caspar, and then explained to the uninitiated, "The Scilly Islands were pirate ports for decades during the era of the privateer. Legend and logic dictate that there are dozens of sunken treasures scattered about the seas of Scilly, each worth a king's ransom."

"Ah, but this treasure is quite different," claimed Dare. "It was never lost at sea — it's been buried — and I have a treasure map."

CHAPTER THREE

Dare Daring To Do Daring Derring-Do

In 1643 Commander John Mucknell began his piracy career with no less bold a theft than that of an entire ship. Mucknell commandeered East India Company vessel The John and marooned her crew on an island in the Indian Ocean.

This was at the height of the First English Civil War, and the parliamentarians had chased Charles II into exile. The king granted Mucknell a privateer commission and the sleek, swift, 44-gun John became the flagship of a pirate armada of eleven ships, with John Mucknell as their vice-admiral of fleet. This pirate navy headquartered itself on the Scilly Islands and became the terror of the English Channel and the Western Approaches, looting and amassing a fortune to rival that of nations.

Then, on the evening of the 19th of July, 1645, while returning home to Scilly after a fat conquest in the channel, The John was met by a hunting party of three parliamentarian warships. Alone and outnumbered and weighted down by treasure, The John nevertheless gave of her best, but took heavy damage. All that...

"...is a matter of historical record," concluded Dare. "What comes next only a few of us know, and even fewer believe that..."

...The John survived the encounter and, mortally wounded and taking on water, she limped home, followed in the fog by the 20-gun Phoenix, commanded by Roger Smalley. The Phoenix was part of Mucknell's fleet of privateers but Smalley elected to not intervene to help The John. Instead, he followed her towards Scilly.

The sea floor around the Scilly Islands is littered with ships that had stronger hulls and better chances, there are reefs as sharp as cutlasses, in some places mere feet beneath the waves. Nevertheless, Mucknell's plan and The John's *only chance was to run aground on Saint Mary's Island. The waters churned and the winds wildly shifted, and* The John *was sluggish and sinking with a hull filled half with gold and the other half with seawater. Finally,* The Phoenix *approached and a deal was struck, the details of which will never be known, but the treasure was transferred to the hold of the smaller ship and* The John *gained a final, slim chance to see another day.*

The Phoenix *was never seen again, at least not under that name.*

Many legends followed the treasure but only one thing was ever known for sure — it was immense. Millions in gold ducats. The most credible tale, though, is that the gold carried the curse of twice-stolen treasure. Distrust and infighting killed off half the crew and Smalley and his officers killed the rest. They put ashore at one of the most distant, deserted, and remote of the Scilly Islands where they decided to bury the gold. The plan was to acquire a new crew who knew nothing of the treasure, retrieve it, and sail back to England where they would divide the spoils and scuttle the ship and become gentlemen farmers.

Of course, The Phoenix *never got her crew. One by one the betrayers betrayed one another, until there remained only a first mate whose name has been lost to the ages, for he was illiterate. This is why he drew a map from memory and shared it with his wife who, naturally, poisoned him. She, in turn, was betrayed by a weakness for gin and a freezing winter. Her son — a theatre clerk in London — made it to her bedside in time to hear her confession and receive his legacy — a map worth millions of pounds.*

But he recognised it for the poisoned chalice that it was. He knew that he could never recover the treasure on his own, and trusting a partner would be a quick cure for living. So, being an educated man, he recreated the map in two parts, one half describing the geographic location, the other the specific. Then he engaged two more illiterates — a gravedigger and an acquisitions editor at Millsip and Hall — to each take charge of a portion. His plan was to anonymously sell the men out to the East India Company for a finder's fee — a fraction of the value of the treasure but more than enough for a young man to live a long and carefree life.

Whether or not the plan would have worked, we shall never know. The legend only tells us that the clever young man was murdered by the gravedigger and that the editor sold his portion of the map for a flagon of Malmsey.

The maps turned up here and there, in antiquaries and bookshops, according to claims of varying credibility...

"...until quite by chance I was competing in a Chinese Boxing tournament in Shanghai," continued Dare. "An old relic of a merchant marine — chap by the name of Daniel Woolacombe — presented his compliments and asked me for a loan of a hundred yen so that he might take advantage of some decidedly worrying odds on my next bout, which was against an undefeated Nepalese warrior whose name translates roughly to 'generous provider of pain and death' or 'October 12th', depending on how you pronounce your 'ng's.'"

"How daring," swooned Teddy. "Did you win?"

"Did I... Well, of course I won," replied Dare. "It was a near thing, though, because against the rules and anything like gentlemanly conduct, October pulled a six-inch rib-tickler from his braid. I still have the scar..." Dare indicated a left pectoral like a flagstone, "...if you'd care to see it."

"I believe I would, yes," affirmed Teddy.

"Is the scar in the form of a map?" I asked.

"Quite right, Anty," agreed Dare. "Continuing with the tale, the old merchant marine never returned to make good on the debt. Instead, late that night, I received a messenger at the junk on which I was staying in the harbour. He didn't say a word, just delivered a package with a note from Daniel Woolacombe, the sailor. The note explained that this was the only way he knew to rid himself of the burden I'd find in the box, for which I'd paid one hundred yen."

"And what was in the box?" asked Teddy.

"The map," replied, as expected, Dare. "At least, one of them was, plus some other artefacts, among which was a hand-written account of everything I've told you, composed by a supposed descendant of the first mate who made the original map. He and his brother had spent a lifetime trying to find the other half. Now, though, he suspected that his brother planned to kill him. It was signed... Rufus Woolacombe."

"Oh, well, bravo," Teddy applauded. "Spiffing yarn, Dare. Literally heart-stopping twist."

"Ack!" deplored Albert. "Figuratively."

Simultaneously, a handsome brass bell above the bar, ingeniously connected to the galley by wires or pneumatic pipes or some such thing, dinged twice, and all thoughts of treasure and maps and Nepalese warriors were replaced with steaming dreams of bouillabaisse and crispy mental pictures of pie.

A peculiarity of *The Ballast* is that few of the rooms are communicating, and to get from the drawing room to the dining room one must go outside where, since I'd last seen it, the weather had taken a turn for the dark and damp. The precipitation was an indistinguishable merger of rain and spray, kicked up by a cold, coast-bound wind, of which the waves were also taking notice. The boat was rocking a bit, and I was compelled to soothe my guilty thoughts of Ivor with memories of cold leek and potato soup.

The dining room of *The Ballast* contrasts stylistically with the drawing room by centuries. It's a proper manor house nosh pit the length of a ballroom and almost entirely filled with a hardwood banquet table with mother-of-pearl inlay, and the walls are a dozen polished panels of oak, each with a depiction in dark oils of the Royal Navy sinking something French. No less than three crystal chandeliers swing and jingle from the ceiling.

But that's where the decadence of days past took a direct hit and capsized. The only staff on hand was Vickers, and he was asleep on a window seat. The table was sparsely set with nothing more than a knife and fork — no salmon knife, no caviar nor soup spoons, no calamari salad fork, not so much as an olive skewer. Just a knife and fork, a napkin, and a tankard, and within reach of those hungry enough to risk it was a platter of hard tack (also known as 'sea biscuit' or 'cabin bread' or 'inedible') and a tureen full of what might have been salted pork, salted beef, or hooves. There were also pitchers of shandy.

"What the devil is this?" Lord Archie spoke what all of us were thinking.

"Quality grub." All of us, that is, except Captain Slapton, who filled his plate with concrete naval biscuits and lumps of tallow with one hand and his tankard with warm swill with the other.

Vickers snapped into the moment, blinked several times and, as he often does on these occasions, stared hard at his surroundings, trying to remember what and where they were. In time, grim realisation came over him with a nod, and he explained, "I'm afraid, Mister Boisjoly, that this is dinner. The kitchen informs me that no plan nor provision has been made for anything else, except preserved, unsweetened lime, for afters."

"Goes good on tack," claimed the captain.

"Goes well," confirmed Albert the meticulous macaw.

"Chef Syds told you to serve that?" I asked Vickers.

"Mister Carvell is not on board," reported Vickers. "Neither is the rest of the usual kitchen staff."

"Oh, yes, that's true," recalled Lord Archie. "They're on leave, too. Minty has assumed galley duty."

"Has he, though?" I asked. "I'm not one to criticise, Your Lordship, but is it really fulfilling the duty of galley chef, pouring a barrel of pickled fists into a bowl and arranging a score of ceramic tiles on a plate?"

"I did the actual presentation, sir," noted Vickers.

"And nicely done, too."

"Thank you, sir."

Lady Charlotte Hannibal-Pool swept through the door at this point. She's a big, robust, country-bred sampling of the quality set, a famous bon-vivant with standing reservations for lunch at Barribault's and tea at Claridge's — dinner, too, if they're doing carvery. She knows her cabernet from her chardonnay and her pinot from her merlot, and she can pair them all with anything from a Munster Cordon Bleu Strasbourgeois to a Mowbray porkie with encyclopaedic accuracy gained from direct and determined experience.

"Do forgive my tardiness, I hope you began the first course...what's this?" Lady Charlotte's face fell. Her entire spirit fell, in fact, and sunk to the floor before us. Her coiffure flattened and her chiffon wrap wilted about her. Her tiara tarnished. Her pearls paled.

"I meant to tell you, dear," oiled Archie, "I gave Mister Carvell and his staff a short vacation. You'll recall, we discussed a brief crew change for the trip to Scilly."

"Oh, yes." Lady Charlotte affected to dismiss the matter, adding a silvery "ha ha ha" to seal the deal as she took her seat. "How delightfully authentic." She gazed at the platter of salted bricks as though upon an open tomb.

"When in Rome..." Teddy pulled out a chair, "...try not to starve to death." And this set off a general trend of grim resignation.

"Some... of this, madame?" Vickers passed behind Lady Charlotte and myself with the tray of petrified pig parts. Our hostess gamely accepted one glob and two shards of hard tack.

"I was sorry I didn't RSVP your daughter's wedding," I confided to Lady Charlotte because, well, why not make a virtue of necessity. "The very idea just broke my heart, you understand." For the record, I laid on two cases of Bollinger's for a sunrise party at the Juniper.

"Of course, Anty," Her Ladyship sympathised. "The news of Winnie's engagement must have been most trying for you. I fondly recall how inseparable you were during our stop in Monte Carlo."

Monte Carlo is a very small city and it has only the one casino. I couldn't have avoided Winnifred Hannibal-Pool in Monte Carlo if I'd been disguised as a fern.

"Well, she's a very charming girl." I recalled her complaining that the roulette ball made too much noise and that the croupier looked 'detached'.

"She will complain, though," granted Charlotte. "This is doubtless the real reason her wedding was called off."

"Her howdy who now?"

"Poor Mister Milliken," recalled Charlotte wistfully. "We were selecting the centrepieces for the reception when he just stood up, said 'one yellow is much like the next, so far as I'm concerned,' and walked out the door. I understand he's joined a monastery in Spain. One of those brotherhoods that doesn't allow women or speaking."

"Fancy that."

"Still, propitious turn of events for you..." Lady Charlotte raised her shandy, sniffed at it, blinked, and put it back down. "Of course you know, Anty, that should you choose to call upon Winnifred when we're back in London you would be most welcome."

"Oh, how jolly. Good to know."

Lady Charlotte introduced a confidential tone. "I know that you're sweet on Frederica."

"Your niece?" I appeared to recall. "Oh, well, yes, one is civil. Quite looking forward to seeing her again, when she makes an appearance, but her father doesn't approve of me, you see, and I suppose that's the end of it."

"Exactly." Lady Charlotte spoke with the casual, quaking desperation of the society pillar, late in matching and dispatching her first born. "His Lordship and I approve of your courtship of Winnifred."

I surveyed the table for diversion and distraction. The captain was discarding the remains of his fifth nub and reaching for a sixth. Lord Archie was smashing up a hard tack with another hard tack. Bunny was carving a portion of salted sadness into what appeared to be a weapon. Caspar's plate was empty and he stared at some disturbing vision that only he could see, hovering just above the table. Dare and Teddy had both picked up their knots of gristle and were eating them with their hands.

I sent Teddy an eyebrow signal flare.

"So tell us, Dare," Teddy leapt to my aid, "if you've only got half the map, what makes you think you'll find this treasure?"

"Because I regard it as a dare," replied Dare. "I never fail a dare. I once very nearly did, deep-sea diving, off Tasmania, but you know, once a shark understands that you're prepared to stand your ground he'll leave you to your business."

"Oh, what tosh," Bunny begrudged.

"In any case," continued Dare. "I have cause to believe that, having found the island, I will find the place."

"Are you seeking buried treasure, Mister Flashburn?" asked Lady Charlotte.

"I'm seeking romance, Lady Hannibal-Pool." Dare cast Teddy a sizzling side-long glance. "Treasure is so often a happy consequence of romance, don't you find?"

"Is there much romance to be found on the Scilly Islands?" I asked.

"Romance is all around us." Dare tipped his tankard towards Teddy. "And it's just dripping off the Scilly Islands, the epicentre of trade winds and global currents, civil wars and political exiles, sea battles and sinkings. For years it was home to pirates and privateers, royalists, loyalists, constitutionalists and kings. I believe that I've chanced onto a clue to what finally became of some small part of that legend, pirate flagship *The John* and her final, richest plunder.

The documents that I acquired suggest that the treasure was taken by another ship, *The Phoenix,* to the Isle of Prospero."

"The Isle of Prospero?" repeated Captain Slapton.

"Do you know it?" asked Dare.

"There is no such place." The captain returned his full attention to his clump of cartilage.

"You know it as Prosperity Skerry," said Dare.

"There's no treasure on Prosperity Skerry," insisted Slapton. "It's a barren rock at the far reaches of the archipelago. There's nothing there at all but reefs, riptides, shipwrecks and sharks."

"And that's exactly where I'm going," said Dare.

CHAPTER FOUR

Times as Drastic as Limes in Aspic

Inspector Wittersham can be quite acerbic, given the right confluence of circumstances.

The sea was comparatively calm in the morning, but the sky remained leaden and moody. A cold, penetrating mist made itself quite intimately known even before I took to the deck to slip my way to the dining room for breakfast.

"Morning, Antics," hailed Teddy. She was at the dining table with Bunny and Dare, and Vickers was dispensing the secret stock of Ceylon steepings and a private pot of marmalade, from his own personal supply, spread liberally and wastefully on planks of hard tack and used in lieu of sugar for the tea.

"You're looking drowned for days, if you don't mind my saying so," observed Teddy, who looked, as Teddy always looks, like she's ready to roll up the carpet.

"I had a difficult night with the inspector," I reported. "He's a steady chap, in the worst of circumstances, and could no doubt handle illness or rough seas or what he regards as rank betrayal by a friend or any two of those in combination, but taken altogether he can become decidedly personal."

"Still feeling it, is he?" asked Dare, prior to biting through a stack of tack with the strength of ten.

"There was a period during the night when the need to kip briefly outweighed the desire to abuse his dearest friends, freeing me to take whisky inventory, but he's awake again and talking openly of mutiny. The others not up yet?"

"Caspar breakfasts with the first gull. He's in his cabin, he says, reviewing some charts." Bunny spoke as though 'reviewing charts' was a known euphemism for 'absconding with the church roof fund.' "Couldn't tell you where the others are."

The door swung open and the tattered and tattooed first mate Minty Moy pushed in out of the mist. "I brung yas yer tea water, though it wants, still, for broiling and leavings."

"I say, Minty," I fawned. "Do you suppose you could organise a spot of sugar for the tea? And, while you're about it, a smattering of steak and stilton pie, a few young potatoes roasted in goose fat, a pint of caviar, and a case of chablis."

Minty folded one arm across his chest — revealing an elaborately and daringly detailed mermaid — and rested the other elbow on it, in turn supporting his chin in thought. Presently, an inspiration waved over a face like a battered halibut.

"I can do yas some limes in drastic."

"Drastic?"

"He means aspic, sir," intervened Vickers. "I do not recommend it."

"Will the captain be joining us?" I asked. "I have what I think are some minor but key hospitality suggestions to put to him."

"The captain'll be along presidently," malaproped Minty. "The others are still on shore."

"Still on what now?"

In that instant the door opened and the captain struggled through.

"Morning, Minty, passengers…" he regarded the table. "No limes, Minty?"

"Minty, do you mean to say that we're in port?" I persisted.

"We was in port."

"We were in port," corrected Albert Ross.

"But not now," I asked, by instinct, the bird.

"N'arr," answered Slapton. "His Lord and Ladyship and Miss Hannibal-Pool wished to pass the night in Hugh Town, on Saint Mary's Isle, so that's where I left them. We be anchored off Grimsby, on the island of Tresco, awaiting high tide."

"There's an hotel in Hugh Town?" I mourned for the night that Ivor might have spent on solid ground.

"Two, if you count the inn over the pub."

"There's a pub in Hugh Town?"

"Three, if you count the Fisherman's Rest," inventoried Slapton, before confiding, "Too snooty, for my tastes. They have French wine."

"You don't say. And what's in Grimsby?"

"Cromwell's Castle…"

"Does it have wine?"

"It's more of a ruin," considered Slapton. "There's otherwise just the post office. It's why we're going ashore."

"Doubtless the inspector will want to stick his oar in, then, not to mention fall to his knees and kiss the ground," I presumed. "Minty, please inform me when we're docked at Grimsby."

"It will be my pleasance, sir."

"My pleasure…" squawked Albert Ross.

"You haven't any essence of wormwood on board, have you Minty?" Dare flicked an invisible crumb from his cuff and rose the table.

"I can do yas limes in aspen."

"Pity." Dare made his way to the door. "It's a ready remedy for mal-de-mer — a bit of wormwood steeped in port."

"I can do yas a nice grog," offered Minty. "Got barrels of the stuff."

"Do you have port?" I asked. "It might not help the inspector, but it wouldn't do me any harm."

"I don't, actually," replied Dare. "I confess I had counted on a more broadly outfitted cellar."

"Perhaps you would do me the honour, Teddy, of accompanying me ashore..." Without awaiting an answer, Dare said, "Till then," and slipped through the door and into the mist.

"Perhaps he'd do me the honour of falling overboard," suggested Bunny.

"I think he's delightful," differed Teddy.

"You think he's tall," countered Bunny. "Chaps like that, Teddy, don't know a thing about loyalty. You saw how he was last night with Freddy."

"Just a tick, Bunny," I braked. "Did you see Freddy last night?"

"After you went to look after your sick policeman," explained Teddy. "We had our bedtime ration of grog in the games room. Dare played Ain't Misbehavin' on the piano and taught Freddy to dance the Balboa."

"He taught Freddy to dance while playing the piano?" I doubted.

"He has a lovely singing voice, too," clarified Teddy.

"I would remind you, Theodora Quillfeather, of your duties with respect to your favourite cousin's interests," I said. "I trust you will step in, in future, and see to it that any dancing that Freddy does, she does with me."

"Make up your mind," said Teddy, cryptically. "I tried wrestling her to the ground, Anty, but she's wiry, and knows a trick or two. Perhaps if you weren't nursing your sick friend you might be in a better position to match your wits to Dare's charms."

"You make an excellent point," I conceded. "Vickers, can you top up that marmalade pot with some grog, zest of lime, and brine, and bring it to Inspector Wittersham's stateroom?"

"Yummy," judged Teddy.

"Old family recipe, Tedds," I explained. "I should have thought of it sooner."

33

Anchoring and calm waters and a night riding the rise and swell of a floating carousel combined to finally grant Ivor a brief escape from consciousness. I nodded off myself and it must have been some hours before he called out.

"Boisjoly," he said in the voice of the war wounded. "Tell my wife my last thoughts were of her."

"Right oh," I agreed. "No hope of recovery, then."

"Unless the boat is literally spinning on two axes…"

"It is not," I reported. "Barely moving, in fact. Very well, then, I see there's nothing for it but extreme action — drink this." I approached his bed with a silver salver on which rested Vickers' marmalade pot.

"What is it?"

"An old family recipe. Handed down from Commodore Horatio Boisjoly, who famously captured and held the fortified wine cellar of Chateau Marçot on the otherwise deserted island of Saint Modis during the Napoleonic Wars. It's a very instructive tale, in fact…"

"Boisjoly, if you have even a trace of human compassion…"

"Ah, yes, of course," I sympathised. "Take a taste of tincture, hold your breath while you count to ten, and take another."

"Why?"

"Within minutes your seasickness will be entirely forgotten."

Ivor stared at me beneath hooded brows.

"You have a cure?"

"It slipped my mind."

"It slipped your mind?"

"What with everything and whatnot," I explained. "Drink up."

Ivor eased into a sitting position and took up the pot.

"Smells like sick."

"Everything smells like sick to you," I reminded him. "Remember, just a sip. It's very potent."

He swallowed a dose and then held his nose for a count of ten, then swallowed a second dose.

"Tastes like sick, too."

"Does it?" I asked. "Excellent. That's how you know it's working. Some people are immune to its effects, but if it tastes like rum, pork brine, orange zest and, possibly, lime, then you're practically cured already."

Ivor nodded. "That's exactly what it tastes like."

"Try standing."

Ivor rose unsteadily to his feet, like a newborn deer on a frozen lake. He shot me a hopeful glance and then traced a slow path to the door. Then he turned and looked upon me as though I was a summer dawn.

"It's worked," he marvelled.

"Commodore Horatio also developed a hangover cure, if you're ever in need, but it's composed mainly of whisky."

"Mister Boisjoly," came a call from outside. Ivor opened the door to reveal Minty across the hall, knocking on my door.

"Ah, there you, Mister Boisjoly," he said. "You asked me to tell you when we were due to dock in Grimsby."

"Thank you, Minty... Have you been introduced? I don't think the inspector's participated much in the social activities on board."

"Not formidably, sir."

"First Mate Moy — we call him Minty — Inspector Wittersham, of Scotland Yard," I presented. "We call him Wittersham of the Yard. Inspector, Minty brings us news that we have an hour on solid ground before us."

"I might just remain on board." Ivor moved about his room, opening the curtains.

"You may be interested to know, Inspector, that Lord Hannibal-Pool is not on board, and that there's a post office in Grimsby."

"Is there now?" Ivor addressed Minty. "Has His Lordship already arranged to pick up the mail?"

"Yes sir," replied Minty. "It's my proverb to collect the mail."

"It's your what?"

"He means privilege," I translated. "Or possibly province."

"I shall accompany you to the post office, Minty," directed Ivor, "and see to it that Lord Hannibal-Pool delivers every single letter."

Grimsby, seen from the quay and taken as a sun-drenched merchant port bustling with the trade of spices and romance, was disappointing. It was certainly peaceful, like a Sunday morning or a moor or a glass of warm water, and quite presentable in the way one wants to see a rugged outcropping of volcanic archipelago, turning a jagged, largely featureless face on the uncompromising Atlantic. There was something of a beach lined with arcs of flotsam, by the water, and a road of squat, sturdy, storm-tested stone dwellings by land. There was also some scrub brush. The only sound was seven bells, struck by Minty, which resonated across the water and vanished without an echo.

Ivor breathed deeply of the sea air.

"Bracing," he declared.

To me the air smelled of wet.

Minty led the way. Ivor and I trudged behind on the sodden quay.

"Strange how unfamiliar it is to be on dry land once you've got your sea legs," observed Ivor.

A boy fishing off the quay directed us to the new Grimsby post office, which turned out to be a corner of a stone storage for nets and rigging, the old one presumably having been a tide pool into which people chucked letters in bottles.

Some half-dozen of Grimsby's labour force were gathered around the door of the shed, busily smoking and nodding, and they regarded us with a sort of bemused pity, the very look that born sailors reserve for those who mark themselves out instantly as freshwater swabs.

"We've come to discard our duty to the Royal Mail," announced Minty.

"Eh?" replied all six of the sailors, in one form or another.

"He means discharge," I interpreted.

"We're from *RMS Ballast,*" announced Ivor. "We have a charter for all post addressed to Scilly Islands south of Gilstone Rock."

Five of the sailors, it should be noted, were young, red-faced boys, taking pipe-smoking lessons — very much in the Socratic tradition — from their elder, a salt-bleached ancient formed mainly of leather and eyebrow.

"There ain't nothing south of Gilstone Rock," sayeth the Elder. "Except Spain."

Ivor, in a surprisingly subtle strategy aimed at gaining the trust of the natives, filled, tamped, and lit his pipe. They observed his easy skill with the universal equaliser with acceptance and admiration.

"Nevertheless," puffed Ivor. "We'll take whatever you have for *RMS Ballast.*"

"There's never a boat called *RMS Ballast,*" doubted the class more or less as a whole.

"Belay all that." The professor of pipology raised his stem. His acolytes fell into a respectful silence. "There is such a vessel. For many a year there've been rumours that she might one day return."

The professor levelled a grave look on two of his more promising students, a clay and a long-stemmed calabash. "In the back, beneath the rigging of the ill-fated *Sea Scout* and the bell of *The Louise,* you'll find an old steamer trunk, marked in chalk and faded hand, *'RMS Ballast'."* Clay and Calabash hesitated, but the old professor said, "Go. Fetch it now." Then he turned to Ivor, lowered his pipe, and added in the low, measured tone in which legends are told, "You'll be required to sign a receipt."

Ivor lingered at the post office to compare techniques and tales of the sea with the class. Clay and Calabash carried the trunk to the boat with Minty leading the way, and me wandering wistfully in their wake. It was no teeming metropolis, Grimsby, in much the same way and to the same degree that Ivor is no Sir Francis Drake, but it did have about it a certain seafaring romance. A maritime wind seduced with the scent of adventure and exploit and distant shores, and the rushing sea and ever-changing sky spread to infinity in all directions, leading from this point on the globe to anywhere and everywhere and to parts yet unknown. It would have been a smashing opportunity to recite a little Coleridge to Freddy, if she'd only been to hand.

There was no one at all on board when we returned, apart from Captain Slapton and Albert Ross. The captain stood on the deck, grimacing hard at the western horizon.

"We set sail at eight bells, whether the other passengers have returned or not," he warned. "There's a wicked south-south-easter got us dead in its sights."

"South-easter," differed the macaw.

"Aye," considered Slapton, before noticing the trunk. "What's this?"

"Mail, apparently," I replied.

"Let's have a look, then, Minty."

Clay and Calabash put down the trunk and handed a key over to the Captain. He bent to the job when our attention was drawn to the gangplank, up which Ivor was dragging a length of chain as though he'd been damned to do so since last spotted.

"What ho, Marley," I called. "Little souvenir of your stay on the island?"

"What do you imagine you're doing?"

"Having a butcher's at the outbound mail," I replied. "Captain's prerogative."

In that instant, Slapton turned the key and flung open the lid and we all stared in disbelief at what the trunk contained.

"One letter?" observed the captain.

"I'll ask you to close and lock that trunk, Captain," said Ivor. "We'll have it open when His Lordship is on board."

The trunk party headed below decks, where the captain, the clay, and the calabash, crowded through a door marked 'store', which was already a clutter of barrels and boxes. Minty was visibly coy about the mess, resorting to stopping before us to buckle his shoe, turning out the light in the corridor, and saying "Got a nice day for it, at least."

"What's in there?" asked Ivor.

"Grog, sir," answered Minty quickly. "Can I interest you in a drop?"

"And who has access to this room?"

"I do, sir." Minty spoke in a confidential tone. "Any time of day or night, sir, should you find you have the thirst."

"Captain," called Ivor. "We'll have that trunk in my cabin, if you please."

This appeared to bring some relief to Minty's nervous condition, and on the captain's instructions Clay and Calabash emerged with the trunk.

Ivor's stateroom, across from and largely identical to mine, was ample for one detective inspector and guest, but with Minty, Clay,

Calabash, Captain Slapton, Ivor, myself, and a steamer trunk, the limitations of life at sea began to make themselves known.

"I'll trouble you for that key, Captain," said Ivor as the party made its goodbyes. "No, if you please, give it to Mister Boisjoly," he amended, as Slapton withdrew the key from his pocket and handed it over.

"As you pointed out, Mister Boisjoly, I'm in no position to accuse a peer of the realm of fraud. And I have no jurisdiction to interfere with His Majesty's mail." Now that we enjoyed the privacy of his stateroom, Ivor set about binding the trunk in chains. "If His Lordship were to chuck this trunk overboard there's little I could do about it." Ivor secured the chains with a sturdy padlock. "Now I've got one key, and the other is in the possession of someone of similar social standing to Archie Lord Hannibal-Pool."

"You flatter the man, Inspector," I said. "It was I who nominated him for membership of the Juniper, and in my capacity as master of the club egg hunt, it's entirely in my discretion who gets to wear the Easter Bunny costume. Similar social standing, forsooth."

Ivor's porthole windows were open, now, and we heard Minty ring out eight bells. Moments later, the engines started.

"The point of this elaborate exercise, I take it, is to ensure that there are witnesses present when His Lordship accepts responsibility for that envelope, and either actually delivers it to the extreme edges of the archipelago, or admits that he's been cheating His Majesty's postal service for years."

"I will be satisfied with him surrendering the charter."

"He'd have to repaint the name on his yacht, Inspector," I pointed out. "I think you have an uphill battle on your hands."

❦

I poured Ivor and me two tall tizzle-and-whisks from my private store of Glen Glennegie and we went up on deck to ride the waves of victory into historic Hugh Town and, finally, the widely-anticipated encounter at sea between myself and Frederica Hannibal-Pool. I posed on the prow, wearing a belted pea coat and an intrepid look, patterned along the lines of Raleigh as I'd seen him last in the National Portrait Gallery.

As *The Ballast* described a wide arc into Hugh Town Harbour, I fancied the all-day morning grey cast me in a mournful, resolute, granite light, and the wind tostled my hair heroically. The salty breeze brought tears to my eyes and I couldn't see with anything like clarity but sometimes the point is to be seen. I smiled warmly and waved with a certain royal reserve at the three blurry figures on the pier.

"Attractive young lady," observed Ivor.

"You have the policeman's knack for the subterranean understatement, Inspector," I congratulated. "Ahoy, Hannibal-Pools!"

"I would have thought you'd have met us on shore," responded a whinging whinny that was worryingly well-known to me.

I blinked away the blur and saw Lord and Lady Hannibal-Pool and their daughter, Winnifred.

"Anty…" oyez'd Lady Charlotte in a mother-of-the-bride broadcast frequency, "...you recall my daughter, Freddy."

CHAPTER FIVE

Not At All A Tall Atoll

Tea time was awkward. Lord Archie had someone else's mail, Ivor had Lord Archie, Caspar and Bunny had a rivalry, and I had the wrong Freddy Hannibal-Pool. On balance, it was probably for the best that Winnifred was among us in the drawing room, filling what would otherwise doubtless have been a conversational vacuum to rival the vast nothingness of outer space with a comprehensive listing of the failings of Hugh Town as a centre of shopping and hair-dressing for even the most undemanding of simple country girls, such as herself. There wasn't even a Russian tea room, apparently, at least not that she could recommend.

Vickers circulated with tea and coffee. Lady Charlotte, Winnifred, and I were fixtures, as mother and daughter had contrived to bookend me onto a bevelled brass bench behind a cocktail table that was, like most furniture on board, bolted down. Lady Charlotte is a stout woman of unblushing appetites, and in the absence of anything to accompany the tea, she was spilling sugar into her saucer and dipping a damp finger in it.

Her daughter is, as mentioned, a top-spinning stunner, right between the eyes. She's tall and curvy as a mountain road and yet somehow delicate, and she and her cousin share sunshine-coloured hair that curls into a thousand independent, springy sprites. However, unlike the authentic Freddy Hannibal-Pool, Winnifred aspires to be more like the equally authentic Teddy Quillfeather, by which I mean rather than leave her hair to pursue its own jolly agenda, she keeps it in a bob that, in her case, looks like a hat made of bees. She gets the flapper fashion wrong in some other key areas as well, and in fact this afternoon she had an ostrich feather in her headband that rendered her, for all practical shipboard purposes, eight feet tall.

Teddy was much more practically wrapped in a full-on skipper's uniform, with white trousers, a captain's cap, and a little sextant brooch on her navy blazer.

Ivor, dressed as Ivor, stood at the bar with a long-cold cup of tea, and I, in observance of Winnifred's presence, had changed into my most unbecoming suit. Of course, I was still sharp as a dapper dagger, but a chap can only work with what he's given.

The captain and Lord Archie and Minty made themselves rare, popping in and out on important yachting business whenever Ivor endeavoured to speak some plain truths about the post. Even Bunny and Caspar, who appeared distracted by some grave development in maritime news, were several times called upon to retire to the deck to smoke cigars.

"We went to see Cromwell's Castle," Teddy finally wedged into the slim slice of silence between Winnie's complaints about the weather and her indictment of the state of the pavements in Hugh Town.

"Do you include Caspar and me in that?" asked Bunny with an easy snark. "One wouldn't have said you'd noticed we'd tagged along, what with you shamelessly swinging like a lemur from Dare's every word." Bunny then addressed an aside to me, "He fought on both sides in Ecuador, don't you know."

Bunny and Caspar had just returned from a lengthy turn about the deck and had brought along an aura of sea air and grim distraction. Caspar, in particular, looked as though he'd spotted a giant squid and didn't want to alarm the ladies. He stayed by the door and pulled his sou'wester about him and stared at the coffee pot as though he'd never seen one so menacing.

Bunny threw off his tarpaulin and posed at the bar, discreetly balancing on the brass rail, affording him a position of advantage from which to lob sarcastic comments about Dare, and to appear taller.

"Where is Dare, by the way?" enquired Winnie with a telling trill and quiver of her ostrich feather.

"Swimming alongside the boat," answered Bunny.

"He's in his cabin. We had to run back to make it by eight bells, but I twisted my ankle…" Teddy raised her left ankle and drew up the trouser leg to display a silk magenta tourniquet, tied with a bow, "…so Dare carried me on his back the whole way, and even then the eighth bell rang as we ran up the gangplank."

"He aggravated his bullfighting injury," added Bunny for colour. "It's still fresh, you see."

"We had a couple of tall cognac and barrel-waters in Dare's stateroom — it's ensuite you know," said Teddy. "Then he chucked us out so he could do Swedish exercises."

"Oh," I sulked, I think, with dignity. "I see."

"I knocked on your door," claimed my cousin in her defence. "You didn't answer."

"I was helping Inspector Wittersham lock up the mail," I explained.

"On what charge, Inspector?" asked Teddy. "Mailfeasance? Mailignancy? Blackmail? Apostasy? Failure to pay stamp duty?"

The door opened and Lord Archie, Captain Slapton, and Minty came in. Archie made a show of pushing the door closed, as though against a terrific wind. Then, with a delivery of such incomparable insincerity that it made his door-closing mime look like Gielgud's 'Winter of our discontent' opening number for Richard III, he noticed Ivor as though for the first time.

"Inspector Wittersham. I see you're feeling better. We're all very pleased. I was just saying to Lady Charlotte how very much I hoped you'd be well enough to join us, wasn't I Charlotte?"

"Much better, thank you, Lord Hannibal-Pool," reported Ivor, as though answering a rote enquiry from a customs official. "I'm happy to be able to report that I have the ship's consignment of mail safe in my cabin."

"Yes, yes, I know." Archie was behind the bar, now, ladling out grog. "Stellar work, Inspector. Most conscientious." His Lordship surreptitiously slid a tankard into proximity of Ivor's elbow, as though hoping he might accidentally drink himself into a forgetful stupor. "Tragic news, though, isn't there, Captain?"

"Eh?" issued the captain from behind his tankard.

"The news," reminded Archie. "The tragic news about the storm."

"Oh, aye." Slapton put his tankard on the bar and glared hard ahead. "There's a fearsome storm coming in from the west. I can see the spouts and shelves from here but what's much worse, gentlemen... she's seen me."

"So, of course, Inspector, we'll have to head back to Portsmouth," concluded Archie, helpfully.

"Is this storm a threat to shipping, Captain?" asked Ivor.

"I seen worse," dismissed Slapton.

"I have seen worse," amended Albert Ross.

"So have I," agreed Minty.

"Not much worse, though," urged Lord Archie.

"Oh, aye," claimed Slapton. "I once nearly capsized, trawling for sole off Squall Atoll."

"Just a tick, Captain." I escaped captivity with an implied promise to return with grog. "Did you say trawling? For sole?"

"Aye. Off Squall Atoll."

"Do I take it, then, that you're a fisherman?"

"Aye." Slapton proposed his tankard as a candidate for refill. "Fifty years, man and boy."

"Not a merchant marine or a pirate or anything of that nature."

"Fisherman," confirmed Slapton. "And sometimes ferryboat pilot, in the off-season."

"And the parrot?"

"Macaw!"

"And the macaw?"

"That be a fishing bird," said Slapton.

"Not really."

"Oo ar."

"Is this in some way pertinent to the question at hand, Mister Boisjoly?" enquired Ivor.

"Just possibly, Inspector," I replied. "Chap at my club, Parker Mintminder, has worn a bowler and a striped shirt for years, he's never without his copy of The Financial Times, and I once saw him make change for a taxi out of the Juniper Christmas orphan fund. And then what do I learn only this week? Not only is he not a banker, he's barely ever set foot in a bank. I feel this is an opportunity to get to the bottom of the mystery."

Ivor gave me that look he gives me when he's quietly anticipating the moral of one of my anecdotes.

"Was that not the question at hand, Inspector?" I asked.

"It was not."

"Ah, well, then, please carry on," I allowed. "We can revisit the matter at a later date."

"It's your professional view then, is it Captain, that we can weather this storm," said Ivor to Slapton, very much leading the witness, if one is going to be pedantic.

"Aye."

"Then we may as well know what we're dealing with, Your Lordship," proposed Ivor. "After all, what with the frequent deliveries *The Ballast* has been making, how much mail can there be?"

"Yes, of course." Archie regarded Ivor beneath hooded eyes and withdrew his tankard of grog.

❧

Ivor, Archie, Slapton, Minty, and I crowded into Ivor's stateroom for the ceremonious reveal of what almost all of us knew to be a single envelope. During the procession, Lord Archie had somehow misplaced the boon affection he'd had for Ivor and, to a lesser but nevertheless noticeable degree, he appeared to be glowering dark thoughts at Captain Slapton, too.

"If you would kindly just get on with it, Inspector," suggested Archie.

Ivor got on with it. He produced his key and unlocked the padlock and pulled away the chains.

"Mister Boisjoly, if you'll just employ your key…"

I recovered the key from my wallet and unlocked the trunk and resigned to the back benches, the better to appreciate Archie's reaction. Whatever I had been expecting — a scoffing 'pshaw' or a fully-realised, House of Lords 'harumph' — I was unprepared for a gape-mouth, wide-eyed shudder of disbelief. It was, after all, only one… dead body.

Inside the trunk, looking dashed uncomfortable, was Dare Flashburn.

CHAPTER SIX

The Import
In Port In Port

"Dare Flashburn has been scratched from the passenger list," I told Vickers later in his below-deck quarters, "and has been reassigned as freight."

"Indeed, sir?" Vickers poured us each a large port from the personal bottle that he keeps on hand for medicinal purposes. "Has there been an accident?"

"If there has, it's the most extraordinary series of flukes of false fortune since Frederica and Winnifred Hannibal-Pool wound up with the same nickname. Cheers." I toasted the fickle fates with a finger of port. "We found him in a double-locked trunk in Inspector Wittersham's stateroom."

Even the below-decks crew quarters on *The Ballast* are comfortable in a close, cosy, tramp-steamer sort of way. There are porthole windows high on the wall, above the water line. The decor is minimalist and practical, and just about everything serves at least two purposes. Additionally, the absence of any actual crew had allowed Vickers to open the door to a communicating cabin and create convincing ensuite quarters.

Vickers joined me at the stovetop card table and pulled up a bootbox stool.

"Has the inspector determined the cause of Mister Flashburn's passing?"

"It was regrettably obvious." I took a restorative sip from my wine/port/tooth glass. "Same old story — chap goes decades boxing Nepalese warriors and facing down sharks and switching sides in a running battle until, one day, he meets his match in a simple blunt object. Same thing happened to Henry Stanley, except rather than a biff on the back of the head it was pleurisy."

"And was there any indication how the body came to be in a locked trunk?"

"The only certainty is that he didn't lock himself in," I said. "Having said that, there's no other possible explanation, either. There were two keys — one of which was in the possession of an unimpeachably reliable party, and I had the other one."

"Forgive me if I'm stating the obvious, sir, but does it not seem likely that the body was placed in the trunk prior to the inspector providing you with the key?"

"Perfectly sound conjecture, Vickers, and you may consider yourself forgiven," I said. "The only difficulty with this theory is that I was present when the trunk was locked, and at that same moment the victim was dashing up the gangplank with Teddy Quillfeather on his back."

"I understand."

"She twisted her ankle," I assured him.

"Very good, sir."

"You have some doubt you feel needs airing, Vickers?" I prodded.

"Miss Theodora is a very becoming, well-bred young lady," qualified Vickers. "But she has also throughout her life demonstrated a mischievous streak."

"I know," I reminisced. "I've always admired her. Do you recall those village fête weekends at Middleditch Castle, Uncle Markham Quillfeather's little pile of rocks in Shropshire?"

"Most vividly, sir."

"Teddy always came prepared. She once placed an advertisement in the Market Middleditch Informer announcing a Lord Curzon lookalike contest..."

"For the very weekend that Marquess Curzon was in residence at Middleditch Castle."

"Exactly," I confirmed. "Simple, certainly, but tremendously original and, I think you'll agree, effective."

"Must indubitably."

"Yes. The drawing room looked like a bumper watermelon harvest." I sipped my port in fond memory. "Oh, and Lord Curzon came in third. She can't have planned that, though."

"On another occasion she rewired all the bell pulls," pursued Vickers, like a hunting beagle on the scent. "Poor Mister Northbridge, the second butler, delivered evening cocktails to Lady Markham in her bath."

"Merely for the record, Vickers, that was me," I clarified. "Although Teddy did stand lookout, and she sourced a vital length of binder twine that made the final leg between my parents' bedrooms."

"I was unaware of that," conceded Vickers. "However there's little doubt in my mind that it was Miss Theodora who climbed the water pipe so that she could paint mumps spots onto Lady Markham's infant grandson with shoe dye."

"That was part of a larger strategy, Vickers, to delay returning to St. Swithun's until after hockey team selections," I noted. "I mean to say, it's not all just for larks with Teddy. She can be quite serious-minded."

"I would suggest, sir, that the anecdote is more telling in the recollection of who was eventually assumed responsible for Miss Theodora's acrobatics."

"I recall only too well, Vickers." I shivered at the thought. "Straight to bed without supper for the entire weekend. I'd have starved had it not been for the nightly hamper of cold chicken, cottage pie, strawberries, lemon coulis, and roly-poly pudding."

"It was my pleasure, sir," said Vickers. "But my intention was to bring to mind the ruse which Miss Theodora employed to escape suspicion of having climbed up and down a drain pipe."

"Well, there you go," I enthused. "Thinks on her feet, if you will — she claimed to have twisted an ankle."

"Precisely, sir."

"Well, to be fair, Vickers, she was ten," I pointed out. "Although, to be fairer still, it's a solid standby, the twisted ankle. Can such a claim even be disproven? Is a twisted ankle even a recognised medical condition? It'll probably turn out to be like 'the vapours' or 'an important meeting at the bank' — just one of those things that people say. In any case, Teddy says that she was with Dare at eight bells, and I believe her, but even if I didn't, her account is supported by Caspian Starbuck and Henry Babbit, who were also present. Dare Flashburn had to have been alive when Ivor and I were locking the trunk."

"Could it all be explained by simple sleight of hand?" asked Vickers.

"I suppose it's as likely as anything else," I acknowledged. "Although, since Dare was last seen alive, I was only ever uncomfortably near Lady Charlotte and Winnifred. I did change my suit but the key was in my wallet."

"And had anyone else access to the inspector's cabin?"

"In fact, that's what I came to ask you," I said. "Have you any idea how keys are distributed on yachts? Is it similar to your average manor house arrangement?"

"No, sir," disappointed Vickers. "Owing to the risk of disaster at sea, crew members typically have a master key for all staterooms."

"Presumably that extends to Lord Hannibal-Pool and party."

"It stands to reason, sir, yes. May I offer you more port?"

Vickers refilled my glass and topped up his own, which I noted also served as a bottle stopper.

"Have you or the inspector formed any theories with regards to a possible perpetrator?" asked Vickers.

"Early days," I said. "And you know Inspector Wittersham — everyone's a suspect. He'll be asking you for an alibi before the afternoon is half done."

"I regret, sir, that I cannot account for my activities at the time of of Mister Flashburn's demise," admitted Vickers, "because I don't know when it was."

"No, good point. Nor do any of us."

"However, I'm reasonably certain that I was in the store room."

"The store room?" I echoed. "What makes you think you were in the store room?"

"I woke up there, sometime before tea."

"How very singular," I observed. "How did you even get into the store room? Isn't it kept locked?"

"In fact the door was open..." Vickers spoke searchingly, as one recalling the details of a dream, "...I believe that I was looking for butter or champagne, or any single one of the simple basics that the Boisjoly gentlemen require..."

"I appreciate that, Vickers."

"And then, indeed, the door was closed and locked. Some time later, First Mate Moy opened it again."

"When was this?"

"I regret, I cannot say." Vickers gazed into unbound ether, like a man walking off a sudden encounter with a lamp post. "Mister Moy was engaging in some manner of stock-taking, in particular he was writing 'grog' on all the barrels with a nub of chalk, and indeed he was writing 'grog' on some of the trunks, crates, and sacks."

"Sacks of grog?"

"This struck me as peculiar, too."

"Did he notice you?"

"No, sir," said Vickers with increasing certainty. "The store room is very dark and disordered, and indeed it appeared to have grown appreciably more cluttered during the time that I had been asleep."

"You must have come to his attention eventually," I concluded.

"In point of fact, no," differed Vickers vaguely. "I felt myself unequal to engaging socially, in the moment."

"You woke up in a strange place and forgot that you were at sea," I surmised.

"In the main, sir, yes." Vickers nodded uncertainly. "Of the various interpretations of the situation that I put to myself, the least unnerving was that I was on a train, and that I was baggage, or that I was being carried by six pallbearers of markedly differing heights and abilities."

"Well then, how did you escape?" I asked, agog. "Kick the door down? Get yourself smuggled out in a sack of grog?"

"No, sir, after an hour or so I noticed the Mister Moy had not locked the door." Vickers looked innocently into the last of his port.

"Only an hour, you say."

"In fact, for a time I was unable to locate the door at all," offered Vickers in some sort of defence. "The store room is entirely without ambient light."

"Yes, I noticed that earlier when it swallowed Clay and Calabash."

"Clay and Calabash?"

"Not their real names," I subtexted. "I just call them that, and they call me Land Fish. Do you think I should smoke a pipe, Vickers?"

"No, sir."

"I'm much relieved," I said. "So, how did you finally find the door?"

"Someone — I expect First Mate Moy — returned and, when he left, he neglected to extinguish the light. It was then I realised that I wasn't, in practical terms, locked in."

"You didn't speak to Minty?"

"I was still unsure of my circumstances, sir," admitted Vickers. "At that point I thought I might have been a young stowaway, seeking adventure."

"Safe assumption."

"By the time I arrived on the main deck, it was tea time," continued Vickers. "And this is why I cannot account for my movements during the unfortunate passing of Mister Flashburn, regardless of when that may have been."

"I think you're probably in the clear, Vickers," I assured him. "You never participated in any Chinese boxing tournaments in Shanghai, did you? You can be frank with me."

"Not to my recollection."

"So, that's a perhaps, is it? Well, we'll not tell Inspector Wittersham unless he asks," I conspired. "Brace yourself, though, that could be at any time — the inspector has ordered our return to Portsmouth."

Vickers assumed a not-atypically confused countenance and raised it to the porthole.

"I think not, sir," he said with confidence. "Though the day is severely overcast, I believe the sun is detectable at that window, and this cabin is on the port side. We are heading south — towards the outer Scillies."

❦

"Oh, what ho, Your Lordship. How goes your lordshipping?"

Lord Archie was on the prow of *The Ballast,* packaged in a thick, waterproof coating, and staring into the mist. I hadn't been looking for him as much as I had been looking for the prow. Initially, I was on course for my stateroom when I heard Winnifred's plaintive cry coming from the corridor, and I had reasoned that the prow was as far away as I could reasonably get without swimming.

"Oh, right. What, uhm, ho." His Lordship struck me as distracted. "Any news on Dare?"

"He remains a poor conversationalist," I replied.

"I mean to say, has your inspector any news on what happened to him?"

"He's not my inspector, as such," I corrected. "He's an inspector for the ages. An inspector for us all. And no, he hasn't. In which direction are we headed, Lord HP?"

"Direction? Oh, yes, direction." Archie gestured vaguely forward. "That way."

"I meant on the compass," I amended. "I should have been more specific."

Archie looked around for the sun. He spotted it as a hazy glow behind a grey veil of cloud.

"South?"

"This is my impression as well," I agreed. "I thought we were headed back to Portsmouth."

"We are, aren't we?" asked Archie. "Which way is Portsmouth?"

"North."

"Perhaps Captain Slapton knows a shortcut."

"Yes, that must be it," I said. "These are his home waters, after all. Tell me, Archers, when was it that Dare asked you about passage to Scilly?"

"I'm not sure. A week ago, possibly. When did you write to me about inviting Wittersham?"

"Ten days ago."

"Then about a week ago," calculated Archie.

"I see. And how did he know that you were going to Scilly?"

"Friends in Portsmouth, he said." Archie nodded in that way people do when they're unsure what else to do with their heads. "I mean to say, it's not that outlandish, is it? There must be people who have friends in Portsmouth."

"I was just wondering if there might be some reason why he chose this vessel over some other."

"Well, because we're going to Scilly, obviously."

"If it would give you some relief to add 'thanks to you' to that statement, I encourage you to do so. Unburden yourself, you'll feel better."

"I'm not sure I'm following." Archie turned his face back into the wind.

"Inspector Wittersham knows that you've never fulfilled the terms of your postal charter," I explained. "And he also knows that the only reason we're doing so now is that I invited a policeman to join us on a trip which, officially, is on behalf of the Royal Mail."

"What were you thinking, Anty?"

"That you were an essentially honest peer of the realm."

"Anty, really," scoffed Lord Archie. "You ought to know better than that. Tell me something, did Wittersham take any special note of the fact that I wasn't on board when *The Ballast* docked at Grimsby?"

"I think he felt it gave him greater latitude to take charge of the mail," I recalled. "Apart from that, nothing of note. Why do you ask?"

"Grimsby is, and for years has been, the single busiest smuggling port in the Western Approaches, and that includes Guernsey." Archie spoke in confidential tones, nearly inaudible above the wind. "So I stayed clear. I don't need the inspector thinking that I'm a smuggler, on top of everything else."

"But, Archie," I made minor contention, "you are a smuggler."

"Yes, all right, Anty, but not on this trip I'm not," nit-picked Archie. "And in any case, a spot of grappa for one's own personal consumption and that of one's closest hundred-odd friends isn't really considered smuggling by any magistrate that I know."

"That would doubtless be because you know magistrates, Your Lordship," I pointed out. "Not to mention the Prime Minister."

"Well, precisely, Anty — this is why I must avoid any hint of scandal," confided Archie. "Do you think you can manage to keep this murder from becoming a spectacle?"

"You can rely on me, Lord H-Pool. Of course you already know about my occasional successes with the police."

"Yes, rather." Archie spoke with a certain small antipathy towards my occasional successes with the police. "There was that business with the Tenpenny Tontine. It was in the papers. I think that's when Lottie learned Wittersham's name."

"And it's when I learned what a tontine is," I said. "It was also the occasion on which I gained Inspector Wittersham's trust — we drew close over tea at Claridge's, during which he accidentally ordered and drank an elderflower champagne cordial, knocked over the cheese trolley, and called the concierge 'your majesty'. And I've never told anyone."

"You just told me."

"I mean to say I've never told anyone that I don't know well, apart from a few cabbies and a columnist for *The Times'* society page."

"Your point being, Anty?"

"Discretion," I said, discreetly. "Also, if you ever get the chance, take Inspector Wittersham to Claridge's for tea. You'll have tales to tell your grandchildren."

"If you could just try to contain your inspector, Anty."

"Again, not my inspector. He's nobody's inspector. Like an eagle, or a highly-sought-after tailor. Nevertheless, I'll do what I can."

"You might do something else, while you're about it, Anty..." Archie's tone warmed by about five worrying degrees. "Look in on Winnifred, why don't you. This whole affair has her quite shaken."

I could believe it. I was with Winnifred Hannibal-Pool when she was shaken by too much foam in her whisky sour.

"Of course, Lord Hannipool. In fact I came up here on the prow looking for her."

"What made you think to look here?"

"Well, I already looked in the engine room, and I was out of ideas."

The fog had been closing around us as we spoke, and it had now taken on that numinous, isolating effect, as though *RMS Ballast* had left the natural world and was floating alone in some celestial bathtub.

The rustle and rush of the wake of *The Ballast* cutting through the waves was the only sound, but soon a peal of the ship's bell came to us from all directions, followed by the voice of the captain.

"T'is second bell of the first dog watch…"

"Ack… first bell of the second dog watch."

"Oo arr."

The captain emerged from the mist.

"On the inspector's instructions, Your Lordship, Misty and me have put the poor departed in an aft crew cabin."

"Ack!"

"Misty and I."

"Oh, right, excellent," esteemed Lord Archie. "Ehm, Captain, in which direction would you say we're currently travelling?"

"Our heading be 184 degrees, Your Lordship, to account for the wind."

"Of course, the wind."

"What is 184 degrees as it relates to, say, north?" I asked.

"South," replied Slapton.

"And why are we going south?"

"The inspector no longer wishes to return to Portsmouth," explained the Captain. "And so we're continuing into the storm, to deliver the mail."

"The mail?" stuped Archie. "There's mail?"

"Aye, Your Lordship. There was an envelope in the trunk, bound for Prosperity Skerry."

CHAPTER SEVEN

The Ennobling Victory of Balthazar Tiptree

"Do I need to remind you, Inspector, that there's a killer on board this boat?"

I had traced Ivor to Dare Flashburn's en suite stateroom and, having thusly cornered my prey, put to him this searching question.

"No, you do not, thank you very much Mister Boisjoly," replied Ivor with an airy distraction. "Have you any other questions?"

"Doubtless you've anticipated it — why are we not returning to Portsmouth as previously indicated?"

"There's mail wants delivering." Ivor took in the larger view of the reception room. It was a sizeable and sleekly styled salon with mitred metal wainscotting following the dictates of deco all around the room. This was matched by copper light fixtures and riveted furniture in experimental materials, and paintings in pewter frames depicting, as they did all about the ship, English victories over French forces at sea. Ivor picked up an immense, broad-bladed knife from the writing desk.

"Curious," I judged. "I wonder what sort of mail Dare was getting to justify a military-grade letter-opener."

"It's a kukri." Ivor admired it against the light. "Nepalese close-fighting weapon."

"Surely this phase of the investigation could be as easily done in home waters, Inspector," I urged. "And, on a personal note, might I add how aggrieved I am to be put in the position of responsible adult. I'm unaccustomed to it. It puts me in mind of wearing my father's greatcoat as a child, with those immense shoulders and endless sleeves and more hidden flask pockets than the royal enclosure at Epsom."

"Captain Slapton tells me that we're in the eye of a tempest, and we won't be able to break through for at least a day." Ivor examined a handsome brass umbrella stand, in which Dare had stored a small collection of swords. "Furthermore, the storm is heading south. In short, it would take us exactly as long to deliver the letter to Prosperity Skerry as it would to wait out the storm."

"You're never going to Prosperity Skerry to deliver a letter," I said.

"No, Mister Boisjoly, there's been a murder," Ivor picked up and tested the heft of a knotty shillelagh, "and a letter found in the same sealed trunk as the body seems to me to qualify as a clue."

"But the letter was already in the trunk," I pointed out. "I recall seeing it — little thing, really, and quite flimsy. Well short of requirements as a murder weapon."

"In fact, it's the contents of the envelope that I find significant." Ivor opened a handsome, silver and mother-of-pearl case on the tea table. It contained a pair of ornamental duelling pistols and a brass plaque, dedicating the gift from Czar Nicholas.

"You tampered with His Majesty's post?"

"I did. In the course of an investigation, such things will be inevitable."

"Very well, and what was in the envelope that you found so very significant."

"Nothing," said Ivor. "The envelope was empty."

"That does, I confess, strike me as significant."

"I thought it might." Ivor moved his investigation into the bedroom and I followed.

"The mail charter held by *RMS Ballast* is for the extended Scilly Islands, those south of Gilstone Rock." Ivor pulled a suitcase from beneath the bed. "There are no postal addresses, as such, south of Gilstone Rock, this is no doubt why Lord Hannibal-Pool accepted the charter and felt comfortable ignoring it. Indeed, there was only the one, empty envelope in the trunk. It's my view that someone wanted this boat to make this particular journey."

"Someone did," I acknowledged. "Dare Flashburn."

"What makes you think that?"

"He told us, while you remained prey to the movement of the sea."

"And did he say why he wanted to go to Prosperity Skerry?" Ivor put the suitcase on the bed and opened it. It contained small stacks of drachmas, dinars, rupees, rubles, and yen, a Swahili/Danish dictionary, a copy of the Calcutta Times with the crossword mostly done, a Turkish regional train schedule, numerous passports, a letter of introduction from the Sultan of Brunei, and a half-a-box of Turkish Delight.

"He did, in fact, hint something about his reasons for going to Prosperity Skerry, now I come to think of it," I said.

Ivor raised himself into cynical position and regarded me with a weary squint.

"There has been rather a lot going on, Inspector," I noted.

"What key piece of information have you neglected to tell me, Mister Boisjoly?"

"Dare thought there was buried treasure on Prosperity Skerry."

"Buried treasure."

"Or treasured berries. There was a lot of grog being passed around."

"Think there's anything in it?"

"I can tell you that Dare certainly thought so," I offered. "And I can add that somewhere in this stateroom there should be a map."

"A treasure map?"

"For lack of a less charged expression, yes," I said. "Note that it's part of a pair — one map indicates Prosperity Skerry, in general navigational terms, and the other the specific location on the island where the booty is buried."

"Which half did Mister Flashburn have?" Ivor gave up on the suitcase and was looking through the drawers of the dressing table.

"Presumably the one indicating the island," I guessed. "It's how he knew about Prosperity Skerry. It's one of a number of artefacts that came into Dare's possession one night on board a junk in the harbour of Shanghai. This includes an account of how the treasure came to be buried and the maps came to be divided."

"Just clothes," reported Ivor from the depths of the dresser. "He had his shirts made in Hong Kong… and Bora Bora."

"It can be a struggle, if you want it done right," I sympathised. "I have to go all the way to Covent Garden. Talking of going out of one's way, what exactly is the point of delivering an empty envelope?"

"I've just said, it's not out of our way," persisted Ivor. "We couldn't get back to Portsmouth any sooner regardless of whether or not we go to this Prosperity Skerry."

"So you say," I accepted with caveats, "but we could much more comfortably weather the storm at the Fisherman's Rest in Hugh Town which, I'm told, has not only an inn but a wine list. I tire of grog, between you and me, and long for the simple pleasures. Have you tried this year's Heidsieck, by the way? I have a case waiting for me in Kensington but I've since heard mixed reviews."

"I simply wish to settle a few details."

"So do I. The sommelier of The Ritz has reportedly described it as 'chewy'. What could that possibly even mean?"

"With respect to the murder of Mister Flashburn," clarified Ivor.

"Even though, as mentioned earlier and as remains a present and pressing point — there's a killer on board this boat with us."

"Yes, Mister Boisjoly, there is," agreed Ivor. "And there's a detective inspector on board with him."

"Did I ever tell you, Inspector, about Taz Tiptree, chap at my club?"

"Possibly. Probably." Ivor responded vaguely, for he was examining the latch of a promising bootbox. "Let's assume you have."

"You see, that's not his real name."

"Are they ever their real names?"

"I mean Tiptree," I elucidated. "He changed his name by deed poll, to better reflect his status."

"I see." Ivor put his ear to the bootbox and tapped it.

"Taz is one of those self-made types," I continued. "He's from a solid, working-class Midlands family. Made his way to London with nothing in his pocket but one shiny brass purpose — to achieve equal fortune and footing with the nibs and toffs for whom his family had toiled for a hundred generations. Now he has a Mayfair address and an influential position on the Juniper darts committee."

"Well…" Ivor paused to give Taz due respect, "…good for Mister Tiptree."

"Possibly you've observed, Inspector, in your professional capacity, the often indelible and always indomitable effect an ageless ancestry of indentured servitude will have on a chap."

"If you mean simply 'born working class in England' then yes, I've noticed."

"Precisely," I said. "Taz was driven to raise himself to the rank of his family's former feudal lords, but he was restrained by an ingrained deference for those he disdained."

"Two sides of the same coin," pithed Ivor.

"Very much the point of the anecdote," I lauded. "After a year in London, labouring his days as an unlicensed bootblack at Euston Station and evenings as a human fan and wasp-keeper-away for garden parties, he had gathered his stake."

"And invested it?" Ivor found the key to the bootbox underneath it.

"Bought a railroad."

"With what he made scaring wasps?"

"It's an exacting skill," I said. "But no, he had one hundred pounds, with which he bought shares in a railway charter — a ground floor opportunity, as I understand they're called in America, where they don't have ground floors, about which he learned while working as a kicking post at a birthday party for the grandson of the Earl of Wicking, who was kind enough to make space in the enterprise."

"Lucky break." Ivor opened the bootbox.

"The charter in question was for a commuter line connecting Chelmsford to Colchester."

Ivor looked up from the bootbox, in which there were no boots. "There's been rail service between Chelmsford and Colchester for nearly a century."

"Such is the power of a lifetime of indoctrination. Taz knew that, and he trusted Lord Wicking anyway."

"What happened?"

"When the full and frankly obvious truth finally penetrated poor Taz's thick, lead-lined wall of naivety, he screwed up his courage, went round to the Earl's London address and asked him, equal-to-equal, for his money back. The earl, via his butler, replied 'ha!' adding, in the manner of the old school, 'forsooth', and the butler gave him a shilling."

"At least he learned a valuable lesson."

"Indeed he did," I agreed. "He went right back to work — took up ratting and performed for a while as a living billboard on Piccadilly Circus, a role for which he learned the accordion and wore a monkey costume and a fez. In no time at all, he'd saved fifty pounds, all of which he invested in Lord Howling's scheme to widen the Thames."

"Not really."

"I'm afraid so," I said. "Then he worked weekends as a dog-flatterer and invented for himself the profession of domestic page, carrying messages between manors in Mayfair and Kensington. It took him only a month to raise twenty-five pounds, which he gave to Viscount Cabbacot for a five per cent interest in his bid to move the Eiffel Tower to Brighton."

"I thought you said that your mate Taz made something of himself."

"And so he did," I replied. "Not in spite of his reflexive veneration of the quality classes, but because of it. In his capacity as domestic page he didn't just deliver messages, he read them, copied them, and in some cases altered them. Within a year he'd built a portfolio of investments based entirely on that which City insiders tell one another. Finally, he had arrived, with an immense fortune, a new name, and a chip on his shoulder that could be knocked off easily and instantly by the meanest of noble, even unto the humble knight."

"Yes, I see Mister Boisjoly." Ivor returned his attention to the bootbox.

"I'm not done," I said. "That was the prologue."

"Surely not."

"It picks up from here," I alleged. "You see, Taz cultivated a reputation at the Juniper as something of a radical reformer, speaking easily during Sunday carvery of the disembowelment of the ruling classes and laying on a reserve supply of guillotines for the inevitable."

"At your club?"

"We're a broad-minded lot," I said. "So long as a chap pays his dues and does his turn on the limerick panel, it's Liberty Hall. Nevertheless, you're not wrong to presume that there were those among the silver-headed establishment who spoke in cloistered corners of instructive reprisals."

"They wanted to teach him a lesson," distilled Ivor.

"And they were in a position to do so. Many of the members from the age of gas lighting and chariots have considerable influence with the palace, and they used it to bring down upon Taz Tiptree a custom-tailored retribution, forged in his nightmares."

"You don't mean to say…"

"Exactly," I did indeed mean to say. "They got him named to the New Year Honours List."

"They had him knighted, the bounders," concluded Ivor. "I assume he turned it down."

"Well, now we come to the moral of the story, Inspector," I said. "He didn't. He couldn't. So deeply ingrained was the esteem in which Taz held the British ruling class, that all his hard-won ire and principles were discarded the moment he was invited to become one of them."

"I suppose character will tell out, in the end."

"Can you say, hand on heart, that you would do differently, Inspector?" I asked. "In any case, in the end Taz managed to bring some of the class of his working class to bear on the manoeuvre, and he accepted the knighthood under his original, sturdy, working man's name, such that he is now styled Sir Balthazar Piggesbottom."

"Not really."

"It's a perfectly respectable name," I said. "His family has farmed the area around Pigges Bottom for centuries, including the town of Pigges Hill and borough of Pigges Barlow."

"Yes, I quite understand Mister Boisjoly…"

"He's a proud Piggesbottom."

"Very good, thank you, Mister Boisjoly," said Ivor without conviction. "Was the moral something about the futility of vengeance?"

"No, it's not, actually, but it would serve, if that were the point I was addressing."

"Then what point, if any, are you addressing?" asked Ivor.

"You want to work out who killed Dare Flashburn before we're back in port," I said.

"That's the moral of the story of Sir Balthazar Piggesbottom?"

"Not a story," I quibbled. "An analogy. An illustrative comparison of two men who simultaneously harbour respect and resentment, in equal measure, for privilege — Taz Piggesbottom and Inspector Ivor Wittersham."

"Could you not have just said that from the outset?" irked Ivor.

"I could have," I acknowledged, "but then I would have had to have found some other occasion on which to tell you that last New Year's honours list included a man named Sir Balthazar Piggesbottom. Are you denying it?"

"I'll take your word for it, for the moment."

"I mean are you denying that you want to identify the killer before we return to mainland Blighty."

Ivor affected to sort through the trinkets and kickshaws of the bootbox.

"Mister Boisjoly, a murder has been committed aboard a boat full of wealthy, upper class, elites like yourself, including a member of the House of Lords and an heir to an earldom."

"It's a yacht," I reminded him. "It's rather in the nature of yachts, in much the same way as omnibuses are full of men who wear bowlers."

"When this boat returns home, these toffs will be back amongst their own, surrounded and insulated by friends and family and codes and customs and clubs…"

"And your innate reverence," I helpfully provided.

"Yes, very well, Mister Boisjoly," Ivor found an ivory-handled fly-whisk in the bootbox and pointed it me, "but here, on the open sea, now I've become accustomed to the movement of the waves, I feel myself on an equal footing with the principal suspects."

"You believe the killer to be one of the passengers, then."

"It has been my experience and, I daresay, yours, that there's one thing the rich desire more than anything else…"

"Their needs are simple, Inspector, and are no different to yours and mine," I assured him. "A reliable tailor and a south-facing balcony in Monaco."

"No, Mister Boisjoly," Ivor set aside the fly-whisk in favour of a promising oak case, "with very few exceptions, what those with wealth want more than anything else is more wealth."

"I think that's a value system with which many of us could identify," I countered. "Although I, personally, draw the line at murder. In fact, I draw the line at getting out of bed before noon — if I'm required to rise with the mist on a cold country pond, I'd prefer to struggle along with my little all."

Ivor opened the case. It was full of military honours, from which the inspector withdrew and examined a service medal awarded to Dare by the Mexico Revolutionary Guard.

"Perhaps, nevertheless, you won't object to helping search this room."

"Not in the slightest, Inspector," I said. "In fact I've already found the liquor cabinet."

"We're looking, as of your late disclosure, for the treasure map."

"And yet, here's a bottle of brandy."

"Very close, Mister Boisjoly," encouraged Ivor. "But maps are typically paper things, with lines and shapes drawn on them."

"Does it not stand to reason, Inspector," I asked, "that if Dare was killed for the map that it's no longer here?"

"It most certainly does," agreed Ivor. "Which is why we need to determine without a doubt that it is no longer here or, if it is, that it's very cleverly hidden."

"Ah. Then it couldn't possibly be in here." I picked up a battered cigar box from the top of the liquor cabinet.

"Why would it be?"

"Because someone's written 'The account of the fate of the pirate ship *The John,* including treasure map' on the lid," I reported. "I wonder where else we can look."

Ivor took the cigar case and opened it on the night stand. It contained a journal and several scattered papers.

"The journal will have been authored by one Rufus Woolacombe," I elucidated. "His brother, Daniel Woolacombe, forcibly sold the box and its contents to Dare for a hundred yen. Daniel and Rufus were brothers until, in keeping with an esteemed tradition dating back to Captain Mucknell's last voyage, Daniel ended their relationship."

"Why?"

"To rid himself of the curse of the twice-stolen gold," I recalled. "I believe that superstition has it that a treasure with such a rich pedigree of perfidy and poor faith can only ever be the cause of betrayal begetting yet more betrayal."

"Probably something to that." Ivor flipped through the pages of mystery and malice.

"I agree," I said. "It's exactly the same with the unseen machine of deals within wheels and silent appeals that a man must negotiate if he's to become chair of the Juniper marmalade committee, only to be driven mad with power."

"Heavy reading, this." Ivor stopped the top of a page with an inquisitive index. "Taken at random, it appears to be mostly about stabbing." He turned the page. "Oh, no — here's a poisoning. And a hanging, although the chap was also stabbed. I wonder why the killer didn't bother with it."

"Implying that the killer bothered with something else, apart from poor Mister Flashburn?"

Ivor turned the contents of the cigar box onto the bed table.

"There's no map."

CHAPTER EIGHT

A Splash of Dash, A Lash of Brash, and One Last Flash of Panache

"Anty!" cheered Winnifred.

"Gah!" I replied.

The Winds of Whinge had blown open her door the very instant I might have slipped past had she not been very obviously listening for me.

"There you are, Anty."

"And there you are," I bravely acknowledged.

"I thought perhaps you were avoiding me," pouted Winnie.

"How did you know that?"

"Eh?"

"I mean to say, what makes you say that?" I veered. "I was just looking for you, in fact."

"Well, I don't know that I'm at home to visitors." Winnie looked sharply away, expertly poking me in the eye with her ostrich feather.

"Oh, well, right oh," I said. "Perhaps another voyage…"

"Oh, very well, come in, if you must." She retreated into her reception room.

"Or we could have a nice drink in the drawing room," I proposed. "I'll meet you there, shall I?"

"It's all just so very trying, Anty." Winnie swooned onto her fainting couch. She'd changed since last spotted in the wild, and was recognising the solemnity of the atmosphere in a black tassel dress in concentric layers, black satin opera gloves, and a plush black ostrich feather in black sequinned headdress. "Make one for yourself, if you like."

A passing compromise, I thought, and set about the cocktail cabinet like a mother bear defending her young.

I handed over a ripe essence of effervescence and retreated to the bookshelf, whereon to lean in a dignified and distant fashion. I was instantly outwitted, though, by Winnie, who fitted a cigarette into a black bakelite holder and clenched it expectantly between her teeth.

"It's the elephant." Winnie pointed with eyelashes like palm fronds at a black onyx flint-and-naphtha igniter of the rough shape and weight of a fully-grown elephant. As I finally contrived to light her cigarette Winnie made room for me on the divan.

"You've heard what happened to Mister Flashburn, then," I said, cynically satisfied to have a topic so ready to hand.

"I nearly died myself, Anty." Winnie looked lolly eyes at me. "I could hardly believe it."

"No, I know. It strains credulity."

"I'm still not sure I do believe it." Winnie held eye contact while drawing nervous energy from her cigarette. "What, I want to know — what are the chances of such a sequence of sorry events happening to just one person in so short a time?"

"You mean, in addition to a blunt bat beamer to the back of the brain-box?"

"That's just the latest atrocity, Anty." Winnie waved an arc of smoke over the whole affair. "Did you know that Papa refused, simply refused like some sort of military dictator, to give me a new Alfa? He says I can just drive the Invicta for another year. And then Mama said that we're not going to Antibes this season because Lady Hackett still hasn't apologised for trying to hire away Mister Carvell while we were in port last year. So we're going to Nice." Winnie gave a little shudder. "One might just as well be in Blackpool."

"An Invicta is a thing one drives, is it?"

72

"And that's been only this week, Anty." Winnie fell back against the divan under the weight of it all. "And you know who *is* going to Antibes?"

"I was thinking *I* might."

"You know my cousin Frederica, don't you?"

"Ehm…"

"You probably don't remember her," guessed Winnie. "She's ever so plain — I mean that in the nicest way, but she will let her hair just bounce about — so you probably don't recall meeting her at Ascott."

In fact, I did recall meeting Freddy at Ascot, and was in a position to confirm that she had been very lenient with her hair, allowing it the freedom of the field to dance in the wind and at one point entangle itself in my binocular strap. Before she'd freed it, I'd managed to wind it around a waistcoat button to such a degree that we had to retire to the refreshment tent for lengthy and involved negotiations. She confessed to me her weakness for baccarat, Shakespeare's comedies, and backing long shots, and she gave her strawberries to a little girl who was crying because her horse was scratched. We missed the third race for laughing, and she gave me the lock of hair that we had to cut out of my waistcoat, and I gave her the button…

"Anty?"

"Hm?"

"I was saying, you won't remember my cousin Frederica, but not only does she get to go to Antibes, she's getting her own flat on Place du Casino."

"You don't say."

Winnie glanced at the open door. "It seems she's mixed up with some rogue in London." She huffed huffily on her cigarette. "Why aren't you more of a rogue, Anty?"

"Me? Not a rogue?" I scoffed. "I'll have you know, young Winnifred, that as a member of Eton debating society I was famous for taking the minority view, including 'be it resolved that Francis

Bacon wrote Lear' and 'be it resolved that cricket should adopt a combat element'."

"So now Frederica's in Antibes and I'm stuck on a boat in the Scilly Islands." Winnie crossed her arms and glowered at remorseless odds. "You know they had nothing but fish on the menu at the hotel in Hugh Town — bouillabaisse, broiled mackerel, smoked halibut steak grilled in garlic and butter — there was effectively nothing to eat. And then Dare is murdered practically right in front of me."

"Eh? You saw what happened to Dare?"

"No, of course not, Anty, I just mean that everything happens to me." Winnie spoke with a withering tone, as one obliged to explain the obvious. "Don't you think that's just a crashing injustice?"

"Oh, indubitably."

"He was ever so dashing, too." Winnie smoked for a wistful moment. "Have you ever considered fighting a bull, Anty?"

"Not for an instant," I replied. "Bulls and I have always had cordial, if distant relations."

"You do write a very nice letter, though."

"Thank you," I said, for what else was there to say. "So do you." Here, on reflection, I might have been more evasive. She did not write a very nice letter, in point of fact, and the only remarkable feature of them, now that I knew they were written by Winnifred rather than Freddy, was how restrained they'd been. I had assumed that Freddy was simply a coy letter writer.

"I dislike writing letters," explained Winnie. "I very much enjoy reading yours, though. You know ever so many words for 'pretty'."

"I do, but I read the Romantics at Oxford," I said, "you should hear me go on about the recurring theme of man's place in nature. A chap should have something to fall back on, I think, should this 'born wealthy' lark fail to take."

74

"You are ever so odd sometimes, though." Winnifred glanced worryingly into that space where we store memories. "Why did you say I had hypnotic hazel eyes?"

I, in that moment, saw that she had blue eyes.

"Because you do."

"They're blue."

"So is the hazelstone," I said. "Very rare. Very beautiful. The exact colour of the Cote d'Azur on a sunny day in August, seen through a glass of chilled Corsican cobalt Sciacarello. I saw one only once, on Bond Street, driving an experienced jeweller to distraction with its obtuse grain. I thought immediately of you."

"That's sweet." Winnie straightened my tie against its will. "I want one."

"Of course you do."

Winnie tasted her whisky and soda and winced.

"Not enough seltzer, Anty." She handed the glass back for reconditioning. "You know I only like whisky for a bit of colour."

"You'd think I'd have remembered that." I desecrated her scotch. "Why ruin a perfectly good glass of soda water?"

"Why do you keep going on about baccarat, Anty?" non-sequitured Winnie.

"Do I go on about baccarat?"

"In your letters." Winnie accepted her glass of dirty water, tasted it, and shrugged the long-suffering shrug of the never-satisfied. "You know I can't abide baccarat."

"Can't abide baccarat?"

"You know that," Winnie reminded me, apparently. "I'm hardly ever bank. It's not fair. If it was even a tiny bit fair I'd always be bank. And bank would win ties."

In fact, I remembered, she had said something to that effect in one of her spartan replies, but I assumed at the time that it was Freddy pulling the long and shapely. After all, at Lady Babbacombe's inaugural exhibition of her paintings of landscapes and/or Lord Babbacombe (it was difficult to say and one can't just ask these things), it was Authentic Freddy who, with only a deck of Happy Families cards and a sly word to the butler, converted the grand piano into an ad hoc, black market baccarat table. This was one of the few occasions in which I came out ahead as bank, too, a victory headlined by no less than three natural Mister and Mrs Saw The Carpenter in a row.

"Ah, well, I recall us playing it together in Monte Carlo," I extemporised. "Remember how much fun that was."

"We never did," contended Winnie.

"Did we not?" I sipped my well-weighted whisky, wonderingly. "I distinctly recollect you consistently shifting my bet to your age."

"That was roulette."

"Was it?" I asked. "Then which is the one where you have to get to twenty-two without going over?"

"Twenty-one."

"Yes, that one. Which one is that?"

"It's *called* Twenty-one."

"Ah, right." I nodded innocent recollection, and then turned my attention to the whisky, a perfectly serviceable twelve-year-old Aberfeldy, probably bottled in 1922, and particularly evocative of its sherry oak casks and the gold panned from its source waters, the Pitilie Burn. "What's this then? Scotch?"

"I expect so. Papa picked it up in Hugh Town."

"Oh, yes?" I feigned casual interest. "Did he happen to pick up anything else? A case of this, for example, or, you know, what-have-you?"

"No." Winnie stared sadly at her sorry seltzer. "He didn't even want to get this one bottle — he was worried that policeman would suspect him of smuggling."

"A not entirely groundless concern."

"Returning to your letters to me at the auto club..." Winnie wandered conversationally.

"Let us leave the past behind us," I counterproposed, "and go deeper into the issue of the menu at the Fisherman's Rest."

"I was puzzled by a poem that you wrote."

"Me?" I scratched the doubtful chin. "Write poetry? I expect you're thinking of some other chap who sends you letters care of the auto club."

"It was called 'A Modest Motion for the Morrow'." Effective whinging is an exacting exercise, and I recalled then that over the years Winnifred had cultivated a punctilious memory for detail. "You sent it on March 2nd. It arrived with the afternoon post, which was fully a quarter of an hour late."

"Ah, yes, I see," I said. "So you suspect that some poet tampered with the mail..."

"The second of the two verses went as follows...
To row again upon the River Thames
To go again much more than friends
To lose ourselves for a quiet snort
In the maze at Hampton Court"

"Yes."

"Anty, you've never taken me rowing."

"My dear Winnifred, you're not giving me credit for those lines, surely," I stood astounded.

"You wrote them," Winnie pointed out.

"Not originally, I didn't," I continued blindly. "I was quoting Shakespeare."

"Shakespeare."

"It's from Romeo and Juliet — you know; 'Parting is such sweet sorrow, so maketh I this modest motion for the morrow'."

"Romeo and Juliet is set in Verona. How does Hampton Court maze enter into it?"

"It's from an earlier folio," I doubled down, "in which most of the action takes place in Twickenham."

Winnie issued me one indulgent smile, redeemable for a limited amount of four-flushing.

"You're very fortunate that you're so cute."

"You've no idea how often I've heard that from magistrates." I mustered all my subject-switching skills to bear before she recalled the limerick poem I wrote to Freddy on the subject of the Winds of Whinge. "Still, cute's nothing on panache, is it? Or dash. I say, talking of those largely interchangeable characteristics, when was the last time you saw Dare?"

"We had drinks in his cabin last night," reminisced Winnie with fond melancholy.

"I say…"

"I mean to say 'we'," clarified Winnie. "Caspar, Bunny, and Teddy were all there, too."

"Oh, right oh, then," I braved the snub with the stoic strength for which we Boisjolys are famous. "He was alive at the time, was he?"

"Of course." Winnie smiled into the middle distance. "Ever so much alive."

"I was under the impression that the evening ended in the games room once you'd mastered the Balboa under Dare's exacting tutelage."

"Why, Anty…" Winnie smiled a flat smile that I think was meant to appear sly, but slipped just over the thin line into nightmarish, "...I believe you're jealous."

"Oh, yes, quite. I'm in a blind rage," I assured her. "Teddy tells me that you had grog in the games room. Was the point of retiring to Dare's cabin to move the evening onto a more stable, brandy-based footing, or is that where he kept his bassoon?"

"He didn't have anything to drink. In fact, I remember that Teddy brought along a pitcher of shandy," recalled Winnie. "We went to his cabin so that he could show us his treasure map."

"You saw it?"

"Of course," offhanded Winnie. "It was right there in the cigar case."

CHAPTER NINE

Bunny Babbit's Billiards Habits

"Yes, I saw the map." Bunny struck almost the exact same note with the word 'map' that my mother does when she refers to my 'friends'. "We all did."

Bunny was in the games room, practising cannons on the billiards table with the cue ball, the yellow, the red, and an effortless wrath. I hadn't been looking for him, specifically, but I felt the games room a likely gathering ground for bright young passengers on a murder yacht.

Bunny was wearing a Little Lord Fauntleroy suit. I mean to say, he wasn't, not even a little bit, and in fact his white serge double-breasted was impeccably trimmed and tailored, but it was just this fastidiousness that made the ensemble appear to have been picked out by his mother. Nevertheless, he lay like a sniper over the billiards table and lined up his cue just as the boat, as boats will, swayed, and he rebounded the cue ball four times the length of the table without touching the red or yellow.

Bunny unbent and watched the cue ball roll back to exactly where it started, and then put words to what we'd both been thinking, "Why is there a billiards table on a boat?"

"Lord Archie got it cheap," I explained. "It's the same reason this boat, his house in Kensington, and his Rolls Royce Phantom are all painted waterproof black."

The boat rolled with the sea and we watched the balls march in a uniform line from one side of the table to the other, and then back again.

"Did you recollect anything from the map?" I climbed onto the officiator's stool to watch what promised to be an entertaining match of man against the elements.

"Looked much like most maps," supposed Bunny. "Yay big, hand-drawn, had some irregular shapes on it. I expect they were islands because one of them had an X on it."

"This corresponds to Winnifred's recollections, as well," I noted. "Although she was able to fill in marginally more detail, such as the observation that the map was drawn, poorly, in ink and pencil, it displayed appalling penmanship, and it very roughly indicated seven badly-formed islands including Gilstone Rock, Sneaky Reef, Squall Atoll, and Prosperity Skerry. The X to which you refer was on Prosperity Skerry, apparently."

"She remembered all that?"

"And that Dare's reception room was larger than hers, and that he paid far too much attention to Teddy."

"Confirmed." Bunny lay in wait for the balls to line up and then like a shot he pistoned the cue, this time causing the red to leap in the air and execute a surprise assault on the yellow, like a leopard dropping out of a tree onto a grazing impala. "You know why he'd been all over the world and skied avalanches and survived hot-air balloon crashes, don't you?"

"Yes," I said. "Because he was mad as the Mad Hatter's absinthe party."

"It's because he was bred for it." Bunny pursued the cue ball into a corner and, not missing a beat, popped the red into the yellow, which caromed off the far bank and came directly back and counter-punched the red where it stood. "He was born in the Malay, don't you know. His father was an ambassador or governor or some other such bung reserved for friends and family of the fixed and fed. And, I mean to say, 'Dare Flashburn'? Why not 'He-Man J. Loaded-Lady-Magnet'?"

"Babbit's a perfectly debonair name, Bunny," I assured him.

"Beats Dunghill."

"Decidedly so," I agreed. "By a considerable margin, some might say. I should think that even Sir Balthasar Piggesbottom would probably favour his odds over a blighted hallmark like Dunghill."

"It's my real name, thank you very much, Anty."

"Is it?" I marvelled. "Since when?"

"Since January 8, 1896."

"What happened on January 8, 1896?"

"I was born Henry Ezekial Dunghill."

"Great Guildenstern's garters!"

"Yes, steady on, Anty." The boat pitched imperceptibly and all three balls rolled downhill in a neat line, and when they were within range, Bunny cannoned the cue ball into the red from a distance of about an inch, creating a satisfyingly destructive 'clack!' "Everyone's got to be called something."

"I mean I can't believe you're in your mid-thirties."

"Oh, right." Bunny watched the balls form and follow a whirlpool pattern in the centre of the table. "Yes, I get that rather a lot. It's not a tremendous boost either, when Winnie asks if I don't just deplore sixth form Latin."

"Who's Bunny Babbit, then?"

"Well, that's me, too, isn't it." Bunny profited from a momentary lull in the currents, but missed the tide and wound up slicing the cue ball hard right so it ricocheted like a bullet off three banks only to come right home and surprise the red with a starboard manoeuvre. "Babbit is the chap who had the decency to marry my mother before falling down a mine shaft in Africa. Felt it was the least I could do, taking on the family name, and I'll tell you this for nothing, it's a solid step up from Dunghill when making reservations at Barribault's."

"You weren't tempted to pronounce it Dungle, or some such?"

"The very next thing they ask is how to spell it," said Bunny, "and then somehow the effect is even worse. Bringing us, by the way, to what an albatross a name like that is when a chap who's got everything else going for him puts his hat into the matrimonial hustings. First thing a girl does, doubtless you know, is try out her first name with your last — 'Theodora Dunghill,' she'll say to herself, 'I think perhaps not.'"

"No. I can see that."

"So, I say, Anty, be a good chap and talk to Teddy for me, will you?"

"Certainly," I readily agreed. "About what?"

"Well about me, you slow train." Bunny trapped the three balls using a second cue as a rail. "About what a top bloke I am, and how I'm reliable and taller than I look even though height, very obviously, isn't everything."

"You don't think the romance aspect of the voyage has been somewhat adulterated?" I asked. "There has been something of a murder."

Bunny chipped the cue ball, lifting it from the table in a spinning googly straight for the Boisjoly bean. I caught it left-handed or, rather, my cricket instincts plucked it from the air before I knew what was happening.

"When you aim for the king, Bunny, received wisdom dictates that you not miss."

"I was trying something out."

"As have better men than you, Babbit." I tested the weight of the ball. "Instruments don't get a great deal blunter than a ceramic sphere, do they?" I lobbed the ball back to Bunny. "Oh, I say, sorry to raise the mundane matter of murder in the middle of a strategy session — what was it I was meant to tell Teddy? That you're a man of depth and sensitivity?"

"Yes, obviously, dreadful tragedy and all that," Bunny repositioned the cue ball and it immediately made for open spaces. "One naturally allows a decent interval to pass, but it's not as though Dare and Teddy had any sort of formal arrangement."

"Did she really ride on his back all the way from Cromwell's Castle?"

Bunny, who had been sneaking up behind the elusive cue ball and was nearly horizontal with the table, dropped his forehead to the green felt. "Yes."

"Because she twisted her ankle."

"It's what she said." Bunny discharged a sudden, pique-powered sneak attack, scattering the balls like panicked villagers. "Smashing timing, if she did."

"How so?"

"The captain had warned us to be back by eight bells…"

"He encouraged us along similar lines," I recalled.

"Still plenty of time, though, and Cromwell's Castle has a rather spiffing view over the straight." The boat and table tilted sharply on two axes, sinking all three balls in a corner pocket. "Accordingly, we lingered a bit until Dare reckoned it had to be coming up on time to go. The Castle's a battery tower on a bit of a rocky shoal sort of thing — the sides are a bit treacherous but easily avoided, and yet somehow Teddy managed to slip off the path. I was inside the tower at the time but it's what she said happened, and of course by then the only way to get back in time was for Dare to carry her, swinging from vine to vine."

"And then you all went to his stateroom for brandy and treasure maps."

"Ehm, no…" Bunny recovered the balls and gave them their freedom. They scampered off in all directions. "No, we saw the map last night. I don't recall it coming up today after the stop at Grimsby."

"And then Dare asked to be left to his callisthenics," I said. "What did you get up to, then?"

"Get up to?" queried Bunny. "What makes you say I got up to anything? We went to tea, I believe. You were there, in fact."

"Not immediately you didn't," I reminded him. "There was some little time between eight bells and tea, if memory serves, and even then you and Caspar were popping in and out."

"He had some cigars that needed smoking, I believe."

"And prior to that?"

"I was in my cabin." Bunny was reduced to idly sniping at balls as they passed, like ducks in a shooting gallery. "No idea what the others were up to."

"So, Caspar and Teddy might have gone off together, you think, for a quiet toot or toddle around the deck?"

"Certainly not, Anty." In rapid succession, Bunny shot his cue at the red, the yellow, and the white, and missed all three. "Caspar was in his stateroom. I'm not sure what became of Teddy but she wasn't with Caspar."

"You just said you didn't know what became of any of them."

"I didn't," said Bunny. "I mean to say, I don't, but Caspar's no cad. He's a puffed-up, privileged pair of padded shoulders, but he's no cad."

"Do cads take walks around decks?"

"Well, it's just not playing the game, is it?" Illustrating the very concept, the billiard balls rolled from one end of the table to the other and then back again. "We're members of the same club, you know."

"Is that the London chapter of the Chaps Who Think They Have a Snowball's With Teddy?" I asked.

"Yes, actually, as you've put it that way," said Bunny. "And there are rules to be observed. It's bad enough we've gone on this junket to Equatorial New Guinea, never mind the late addition to the passenger list of Alan Poxing Quartermain and, of course, his tragic demise. It was just meant to be Caspar and me on an even pitch. I introduced them, you know."

"Caspar and Teddy?"

"Yes." Bunny watched the line of balls pass him, all in a row, like a little train. "We were making up the numbers at the village fête, on your uncle's spread in Berkshire. Teddy spotted Caspar being pompous as only he could be at, of all things, the coconut shy. She grabbed me and told me to play along and before I knew what was happening she'd introduced me to Caspar as Mats Gilespie, America's current reigning skittles and coconut shy champion."

"But you already knew each other."

"He was there as my guest," confirmed Bunny. "But, such is the strength of Teddy's personality, we played along. In fact, when she subsequently introduced Caspar to Bishop Major Blessing as Bishop Major Blessing, *he* played along. Anyway, once the dust had settled, we were both hatters for Teddy and agreed to let the better man win, no revisals or reprisals."

"Has Teddy any say in all this?" I wanted to know.

"That's what 'the better man' means, isn'it?" replied Bunny coolly. "But one can't mount much of a campaign in London — Teddy's rarely where she's expected to be in the metropolis. I once tracked her from the Criterion to the Café de Paris to the Embassy Club, The Blue Lagoon, 43, the Piccadilly Hotel, and then back to the Criterion, only to find I'd been following some American cousin, to whom Teddy had loaned her memberships for the night. And do you know where Teddy was the whole time?"

"Following you in a taxi with an entourage, making book on where you'd go next?"

"How the devil did you know that?"

"I was in the taxi," I revealed. "I've only just now learned how she managed it."

"So you can see why this voyage around the Isle of Wight, with an evening in Ventnor scheduled for a rose moon, figured so prominently in our plans," summarised Bunny. "Caspar sorted the voyage with His Lordship and I got Teddy's mother to apply the thumb screws. Then Caspar and I settled the ground rules and that's how I know he wasn't on deck with Teddy after we left Dare's cabin this afternoon."

"But you can't speak for anyone else who might have gone to see Dare, or who he might have chosen to visit for reasons of his own," I concluded.

Bunny was crouched behind the southwest corner pocket, patiently skulking the cue ball as it wandered into range, oblivious to the danger. "What's all this about then, Anty? You must know who did it for Dare."

"You flatter me, Bunny. I don't."

"Well, it was very clearly that Minty bloke, wasn't it?"

"Was it?" I asked. "How do you come to know this?"

Bunny pounced, but the cue ball danced just out of range before he could pull the trigger.

"How do you not, Anty? I mean to say, just look at the chap. He has a tattoo of a severed hand holding a dagger cutting the throat of a skeleton... on his neck."

"I should think that you, among all of us, would be the slowest to judge appearances."

"Now just what the devil is that supposed to mean?"

"It means, apparently, that all your talk about egalitarianism and the birthright of the honest poor is all so much piffledash," I ruled from my referee chair.

"It's not just that," Bunny tactically retreated. "You know, he went off somewhere when we were at Grimsby."

"I do know that, Bunny," I said. "He was with me and Inspector Wittersham, collecting the mail."

"Oh, right. Well, I still don't trust that blighter." Bunny stalked the wily cue ball around the table. "He knew Dare, you know. I happened to overhear them on deck, whispering. There's something about whispering, isn't there, that makes a chap listen even when he ought not."

"And what did you hear?"

"Minty," said Bunny in the tone of one stating the obvious. "It sounded like he had Dare backed into some sort of sticky spot, and Minty was telling him he could have a share, if he kept his mouth shut."

Bunny had tracked the cue ball to the far eastern reaches of the table, such that his back was to the door as it opened. "You can take my word for it, Anty, First Mate Minty is a pirate and a killer."

Minty, of course, was at the door.

"If it was to I which you was alluring," said the first mate with calm dignity, "it is so there is much truth a man can say in benigning my repudiation, but I can insure, sir, you that I ain't no pirate."

CHAPTER TEN

The Power of the Pledge Between Hightower and Hedge

"I ain't never killed no one, Mister Boisjoly." Minty waited for Bunny's departure before making this claim. "Not this trip, leastways."

"And who can blame you? You must have a hundred other things to do on board."

"I does everything but steer the ship." Illustrating the point, Minty set about securing the games room, starting with rolling the billiard balls into their pockets.

"When did you last speak with Mister Flashburn?" I casually and, I think, nimbly shifted the theme from murder as a general concept to the murder under current consideration.

"I don't know that I ever did speak to the gentleman…" Minty, stood on a chair to pluck darts out of the ceiling, paused to squint into a middle field of lies.

"You spoke to him yesterday," I reminded him. "I was there. He asked if you had any wormwood and you proposed grog. Disappointment ensued, followed by inspiration and, in time, healing."

"Aye." Minty nodded and smiled in recollection of the happy occasion. "I revoke the equation — that was when I last spoke to Mister Flashburn."

"Quite sure?"

"Oh, yes." Minty nodded emphatically from behind the bar, where he'd gone to retrieve the quoits rings. "I remember, because that's when he asked me if there was any wormwood on board, which there ain't. Probably why the memory sticked with me."

"You'll want to be quite certain of your movements when you recount them to Inspector Wittersham, Minty," I counselled. "He can be quite exigent when the matter is murder or, for some reason, defrauding His Majesty's post."

"I didn't kill nobody…"

"This trip."

"…this trip," agreed Minty. In a lower, confidential tone he added, "You ask me, it was that Mister Babbit."

"Bunny?" I boggled. "What makes you say that?"

"'Cause he thinks I done it." Minty spoke with a tone of wounded pique. "Seems only fair. Squid pro quo."

"Ah, yes, but Mister Babbit is basing his suspicions on a scientific study of your tattoos."

"So am I basing my suspenders on science," said Minty with cool pride as he harvested table tennis balls from the cushions of the divan. "The science of hearing Mister Babbit tell Mister Starbuck that it would be best for all concerned if Mister Flashburn were to fall overboard and be eaten by sharks."

"Yes, I've heard Mister Babbit express similar sentiments myself," I agreed. "You'd be advised to be equally forthcoming."

"I have done," swore Minty from beneath the billiards table where he was collecting skittles pins. "'Pon my Dover sole."

"You know, Minty, you put me in mind of a chap at my club, the Juniper. Do you know it?"

"I don't believe I do, sir, no."

"Well, I can recommend it unconditionally should you find yourself dissatisfied with your current gentlemen's club," I endorsed. "But returning to the subject of Hedge Sedgley — that's not his real name, of course, but it's something starting with S — this chap at my club. It came to pass one day last year that Gust Hightower, another chap at my club, asked Hedge to keep a confidence."

"I see." Minty nodded knowingly. "A confidence you say."

"What you might call a compliance, or a competence," I clarified. "Let us agree that Gust asked Hedge to keep a secret."

"Done," assented Minty, and then surmised, "And when this Sedgley chap repealed the secret, Mister Hightower slit his throat for him."

"Eerily close," I said, "but no. In fact, Hedge didn't reveal the secret at all. On the contrary, he was honoured just to have been acknowledged never mind confided in by no less lofty a clubman than Gust Hightower, legendary tippleman and founder of the Longfellow Society, an umbrella organisation agitating for a legally mandated cocktail hour and the lengthening thereof to sunrise, and a national drinking song."

"I'm partial to Yo Ho Ho."

"I'll be certain to convey your views," I assured him. "Although Gust's influence in this and other areas has diminished appreciably, all owing to Hedge's commitment to his promise."

"It's always a poor idea, in my expedience, to place too much importance on your world of honour."

"A lesson Hedge himself learned not an hour later when Ample Merriwether…"

"Another chap at your club?"

"Yes, another chap at my club," I confirmed. "Ample arrived in the lounge of the Juniper with a bottle of absinthe, recently smuggled from the continent, and he wanted the barman to use it as a base upon which to compose a pitcher of A Spell Down the Well which, doubtless you know, is one part absinthe, two parts champagne, a single drop of bitters, and lime round the rim."

"Sounds most appetisory."

"It's very much prey to context," I equivocated. "You don't want one before a court appearance or climbing stairs, but yes, it can be quite palatable. Ample, however, insisted that the barman use lemon instead of lime and leave out the bitters altogether, which of course would make it a Pitcher of Dorian Gray — a perfectly serviceable cocktail but not A Spell Down the Well. Ample disagreed, and it was proposed that Gust be brought in to make a ruling."

"I fear, Mister Boisjoly…" Minty cocked his head in thought, "…I may have to shortly rake my leaves — the engines want stoking roughly every six hours, and I had only just done it when I come in here."

"The story is coming within sight of the point," I said, shamelessly. "Enquiries were made, you see, and Hedge, so preoccupied was he with not divulging what Gust had told him, began saying practically anything else that came to mind. He diverted, he dodged, he dissembled, and then finally claimed that it was no good asking Gust Hightower about cocktail recipes, because he'd taken the pledge."

"The pledge?"

"Hedge claimed that Gust had given up drinking," I clarified. "The result, obviously, was bedlam. A hue and holler tolled through the hills and valleys of Mayfair — Gust Hightower was no more the voice of authority and the friend in Whitehall to the honest tipple."

"I thought you said that Mister Sedgley never told."

"He didn't," I said. "That wasn't the secret. That's just what Hedge blurted out in place of revealing the real secret or simply keeping his yap strapped."

"And what was the real secret?"

"Gust had told Hedge 'Don't tell Boisjoly I'm here.'"

"Oh."

"But by then the damage had been done," I eulogised. "To paraphrase Swift, falsehoods fly from pole to pole while the truth is wondering how its shoes got on the roof."

"So very true, that." Minty nodded sagely.

92

"His reputation was in tatters," I continued. "By the end of the day, the Longfellow Society had lost half its numbers and the Barleymow faction had mounted all but a coup d'état."

"No!"

"Yes!" I countered. "Hard to recover from a thing like that."

"Well, I thank you for that, Mister Boisjoly, it was a most humidifying tale." Minty shook his head slowly, as though in awe of the icy indifference of destiny, and continued sweeping up Bagatelle pegs. "But did I understand you to say that there was a point?"

"You did," I said. "The point is that when you said that you didn't speak to Mister Flashburn today you, like Hedge Sedgley, were being something other than truthful."

"You think I'm lying."

"In a word."

"Could you not have just said that?"

"As our acquaintanceship grows, Minty, and we come in time to be, I hope, friends, you'll know that the answer to that is always no."

"I stand by my earlier statesman."

"Would you care to hear how I came to become master of the Juniper egg hunt?" I asked. "It's a most illustrative tale…"

"I spoke to Mister Flashburn this afternoon, after we all come back from Grimsby."

"And what did you discuss?"

"I don't think I can recall…" Minty furrowed his brow in a fibby manner.

"It was treasure," I reminded him. "You were discussing treasure. Buried pirate treasure, to give it its full buckle of swash, and you were offering Mister Flashburn a share thereof."

"Oh, no, Mister Boisjoly…" Minty raised his hands, revealing a diptych tattoo on his wrists spelling out 'What goes around…' '…comes aground'. "I mean to say, yes. We talked about buried treasure, but it were me that was asking Mister Flashburn for a share."

"And why did you feel entitled to a share of the treasure?"

"It's buried, isn'it?" pointed out Minty. "I thought I might help dig it up."

"I see," I paltered. "And did you and Mister Flashburn arrive at a satisfactory distribution of toil and treasure?"

"Nar," Minty moaned. "Mister Flashburn wasn't deposed to the arraignment."

"He felt that he didn't require a collaborator of your calibre?" I surmised.

"Nar — he already had a partner on board *The Ballast.*"

The sea was beginning to express a churlish, mirthless, restless mood and I rebounded off the walls like a billiard ball as I rolled to Ivor's stateroom, wherein to apprise him of the rumour of Dare's secret conspirator. He wasn't replying to a knock, though, so I popped into my own cabin for a risky whisky briskly.

I was just getting to the whisky bit when there was a regimental knock on the hatch. I opened to find Caspar standing as though he expected the king to leap out and pin a medal on his tunic.

"What ho, Cap." I wheeled back and brought the door with me, freeing enough space for Caspar and his shoulders.

"Evening, Anty." Caspar marched in, his hands astern and a dark cloud visible off the bow.

"Tipple and mist?" I offered, holding up my own glass as a demonstration model.

"Uh, no, thank you, Anty." Caspar wandered the edges, inspecting my quarters. "Just popping in, really, to find out if there had been any developments."

"There have, as it happens," I said. "You'll want to sit down for this — I've been writing love letters to the wrong girl for six months."

"I was referring to the murder investigation."

"That's doubtless because you don't know the enormity of the situation," I advised him. "The girl in question is Winnifred Hannibal-Pool, and these letters include poetry."

"You're between the devil and the deep blue sea," adjudged Caspar with a cool detachment that would have done him well had we been strangers or mild darts rivals.

"She has a trying habit of inventorying and memorising faults and flaws," I said. "But I don't know that I'd go so far as to compare her to the deep blue sea."

"It's a nautical expression, dating from the 17th century," explained Caspar. "The devil is a seam running the entire length of a ship's hull, and it regularly wants sealing with pitch. The only way to do that is to suspend a crewman over the side."

"Too late for that, I'm afraid." I reclined on the divan with my whisky. "She's already read the letters."

"Returning to the matter of the passing of Mister Flashburn, Anty." Caspar chose to remain standing. In fact he chose to remain standing against the wall like a floor lamp.

"Oh, well, you know, not a great deal to say that I'm quite certain that I can say." I swirled my whisky coyly. "Have you spoken to Inspector Wittersham?"

"I have. Did you really give him a seasickness remedy?"

"I did," I confirmed. "Old family recipe."

"And it actually works?"

"You saw the man."

"I've always understood that there was no such thing as a cure," mused Caspar. "I regard myself as something of a swot regarding most things nautical. What's in it?"

"I can't really recall, in point of fact," I confessed. "Doesn't matter, particularly, though — it's a placebo."

"A sawbones' bitter?"

"No, a placebo," I explained. "The only active ingredient is wit."

"A sawbones' bitter is an old naval trick," said Caspar. "It refers to the mix of seawater and bilge that would be employed when there was no more rum to serve as an anaesthetic during an amputation. The analgesic effects were entirely psychological. Rather lost its efficacy once it acquired a name, I expect."

"Ah. Then, yes, it's a sawbones' bitter. The cure is entirely in his head."

"Pity."

"I know, but at least we have a fully operational inspector on board to manage the procedural aspects of a murder investigation," I pointed out. "I typically provide colour commentary."

"And I could provide the naval expertise you both lack," proposed Caspar. "I can tell you, for instance, that this story of buried treasure is almost certainly a hoax."

"That's disappointing. Why do you say that?"

"Well, it just doesn't hold water, does it?" Caspar continued his cabin inspection. "Mucknell takes on three parliamentary frigates and a total of eighty guns, and somehow not only survives the encounter but leaves all three ships mastless and adrift. Then he slips two more rebel skips and tacks back to Scilly with timbers so shivered that he's obliged to blast his ballast just to achieve the buoyancy to run his ship aground."

"Well, when you put it like that…"

"And yet there was leisure enough to transfer a fortune in gold to another ship," continued the prosecution. *"The Phoenix,* which, it bears emphasising, didn't exist — there was no such ship in 1645."

"You know a dashed great deal about it all," I observed.

"It's something of family tradition, matters maritime."

"I was referring to this particular Mucknell matter."

"Ah, yes, quite." Caspar, gliding his eye along the wall to a particularly dire representation of the Battle of Quiberon Bay, briefly lost his balance. "The Starbucks have been matelots for generations. There was at least one Master Starbuck among the crews that clashed that day. It's all family lore, to me."

"So Pirate Admiral John Mucknell went down with his ship, then, did he?"

"No…" Caspar considered this from an angle, as he tried to align the horizon with the carnage in a depiction of the Glorious First of June. "No, in fact within a few months he was in command of a 24-gun frigate, *The Mary,* and once again the scourge of channel shipping."

"Then what became of the treasure, if the legend isn't true?"

"Mucknell was a privateer," explained Caspar. "He had a commission from King Charles I. This was during the First English Civil War, between royalists and parliamentarians. Privateers were plundering on behalf of the king."

"So the king got it all…" I settled a sceptical eye on him. "I see."

"Stands to reason." Caspar dodged my darts of doubt and marched across the room to admonish an oil painting of the Action at Cherbourg which had been lolling lazily to one side. "Certainly Mucknell didn't have it, and after he disappeared somewhere off the Spanish Main his wife was forced to petition Charles II for a pension."

"There was a Mrs Pirate?"

"This strikes you as odd?"

"It does a bit, actually, yes," I realised. "Just the one?"

"He was a privateer, Anty, not a Frenchman."

"Was the union blessed?"

Caspar was now studying the state of my portal windows. "No." He tested the rim for dust with a finger. "Or, rather, who's to say?" He closed the curtain conclusively. "There was talk, within family and navy circles, you understand, that any offspring had changed the family name to some variation of Mucknell, to avoid immediate association with a pirate but to keep open the option of staking a claim, should his legacy ever be rehabilitated."

"Quite certain you won't take a drink, Capstan old man?" I asked. "Or at the very least take a seat. You must be exhausted from your inspection tour."

Caspar stood in the centre of the room, his arms crossed and his countenance crosser, as though on the bridge of his flagship galleon.

"What do you make of this inspector swab, Anty?"

"I often make of him a tightly wound coil of crackling nerve endings," I said. "Our friendship is very much an exercise in the creative dialectic. Why do you ask?"

"Why do I ask?" boggled Caspar. "There's been a murder, Anty. There's a killer on board even as we speak. You don't think it notable that there's also not only a rank outsider but a rank outsider with…" Caspar lowered his voice and assumed a piercing, conspiratorial demeanour, "…mal-de-mer?"

"Inspector Wittersham?" I all but sang soprano. "You suspect Inspector Wittersham of murder?"

"Why not?" asked Caspar coolly. "He suspects me."

"He's a policeman," I pointed out. "He suspects everyone. If he doesn't, they make him go back and do it again."

"He kept asking me to account for my actions from when we embarked from Grimsby," recounted Caspar, as though recalling a bitter encounter with an insubordinate midshipman. "And this was after I told him that I'm Royal Navy."

"That's probably got something to do with it," I said. "The inspector has patchily egalitarian views. What did you tell him?"

"The truth, obviously, Anty. I told him I was in my cabin."

"But, you weren't in your cabin."

"I most certainly was," insisted Caspar. "I don't mean the entire afternoon. We went to Dare's stateroom for a bit…"

"A bit of brandy," I helpfully provided.

"Yes, a bit of brandy, I recall, and then I retired to my cabin," testified Caspar. "You may ask Bunny, if you feel unable to bring yourself to accept my word."

"Bunny was with you?"

"He was." Caspar's attention seemed to shift to something that only he could see, somewhere on the mainland. "We have a gentlemen's arrangement. I was simply seeing that he kept to the terms."

"You're neither of you to attempt to dazzle Teddy Quillfeather until and except for the allotted time and conditions," I divined.

"He told you, did he?"

"He did," I admitted. "You don't trust him?"

"Of course not." Caspar gestured, subtly, at his own good self. "Look what he's up against."

"Yes, I see your point."

"Poor chap."

"And you're quite sure that you can confirm one another's movements from when we returned from Grimsby?" I said, measuring him out a metaphorical length of rope with which to hang either his or Bunny's testimony from the yardarm.

"Quite sure." Caspar nodded, his eyes solemnly closed. "In any case, whoever killed Dare was after this mythical treasure, I think we can agree."

"We can, but only because I'm so agreeable."

"Then that lets Bunny out, too, doesn't it?" contended Caspar. "He knew as well as did I that the treasure story was so much bilge. And I tell you something else, Anty — do you know who else thought the whole thing was just a hoax?"

"Who?"

"Dare Flashburn."

CHAPTER ELEVEN

Murmurs Made of Murders Made by Mermaids

I followed the scent of Ivor's pipe, floating on the air like the delicate perfume of a barn fire, to the bow of *The Ballast*. The fog was now the rough density of a glass of milk and it swirled about the feet like suspicious poodles. The evening air was cool and still and quiet, save for the creak and squeak of ropes and rigging, and the shush and rush of waves and wake split against the hull.

"What ho, Amerigo," I ahoyed. "What have you discovered?"

"Evening Boisjoly." Ivor acknowledged me with a puff of smoke and then returned his attention to the foggy beyond. "Not a great deal. I'm not sure I don't know less now than when the investigation began."

"I know the feeling," I sympathised. "One habituates."

"The essential problem is that literally everyone could have done it." Ivor puffed up a contribution to the mist. "And no one could have. It's an impossible murder that anyone could have committed. Clearly, the only way to identify the killer is to work out how he did it."

"It's not as though we've never found ourselves in this position before."

"Yes, I know." Ivor exhaled a grudging gust. "Very well — how was it done?"

"I have no idea."

"You don't know either?"

"I do not," I confessed. "I'm working on a theory — very rudimentary, you understand, but what are your views on mermaids? I mean to say, in terms of whether or not they exist."

"They don't."

"Quite sure?" I pursued. "I have a cousin who claims to have seen one, once. Several, in fact, on our uncle's duck pond in Berkshire. Mischievous devils, if there's any truth to it — they capsized the gondola which, you can take it from me, is practically impossible to do deliberately, and they left what must have been a dozen whisky bottles floating in the pond."

"Lord and Lady Hannibal-Pool claim to have been together constantly," continued Ivor, very much in the vein of these city-bred mermaid-sceptics, "but for when His Lordship was seeing to ship's business, when the captain alibis him. For his part, the captain says that he was always in the company of someone, most particularly First Mate Minty Moy, since departure from Grimsby. Mister Moy agrees."

"Caspar says that he was with Bunny, but Bunny tells a slightly different tale," I pointed out.

"Yes, I took note of that," said Ivor. "But no one person's account matches exactly that of another. Winnifred Hannibal-Pool says that she was with Theodora Quillfeather, but Miss Quillfeather says that she can't recall where she was."

"And, unusually, I note that almost everyone seems to have an idea who did it," I said.

"Yes, I noticed that myself," puffed Ivor. "Lord Hannibal-Pool thinks it might have been you, by the way."

"Not really."

"If it's any help, he's sure it was a drunken accident."

"Oh, well then, fair enough," I accepted. "Caspar thinks it's you."

"Me?"

"That's the precise tone I took and, I assume, which you took when Lord Archie accused me," I said.

"Quite nearly, yes," claimed Ivor. "Lady Hannibal-Pool thinks it was the captain. Her daughter could only suggest that whoever it was, he did it just to spite her."

"Bunny thinks it was Minty," I added to the collection. "And Minty thinks it was Bunny."

"The captain thinks it might have been Minty, too, actually," said Ivor. "But he can't get past the fact that they were together since Grimsby."

"Who does Teddy think did it?" I asked. "She has keen instincts for these things, Inspector, and as a child showed a remarkable aptitude for Squeak Piggy Squeak."

"Pirates."

"Pirates, you say," I pondered. "Think there's anything to it?"

"No, of course not, but there is the whole matter of buried treasure." Ivor briefly gave the notion the smoke test. "Pirates are certainly involved, at least tangentially."

"Caspar doesn't think so."

"Mister Starbuck also believes that I'm a viable suspect," said Ivor. "I'm not very inclined to give his theories much weight."

"No, quite right, too," I agreed. "As a judge of character the man's practically a judge. However he said that Dare himself didn't believe there was any treasure."

"He did?"

"As Caspar tells it, he told Dare that he thought the whole thing was a legend at best and, most likely, a hoax," I recounted. "And he says that Dare agreed with him."

"Then why did he want to go to Prosperity Skerry?"

"The very question I asked Caspar," I replied. "Who said that Dare *didn't* want to go to Prosperity Skerry, particularly. He was happy to have a look, so long as *The Ballast* was going that way, but the more he read of the journal — the one he acquired in Shanghai — the less he believed that there was ever a ship called *The Phoenix,* a betrayal, or any treasure at all. And in any case he only had one of the famous two maps."

"So he wouldn't have been able to find the treasure anyway," deduced Ivor.

"Apparently not."

"We'll have to take a look at that journal ourselves."

A cold westerly wind chased the fog from the deck, unveiling the moon which loomed like a lone street lamp and raised the choppy waves in black and white relief.

"That reminds me, Boisjoly — I'll be needing more of that seasick medicine."

"You who hoo, now?"

"I've taken almost all of it. I'm well enough for now, but when you have a moment I'd very much appreciate another jar."

"I'll do my best to remember," I assured him.

"Much obliged." Ivor hauled in the rigging of his trenchcoat. "Slapton tells me this cold westerly is a sign that the storm is descending upon us."

For the moment, though, the wind was raising the curtains on a crisp, grey and greyer horizon of sea and sky, slenderly delineated by a burning thread of sunset to starboard. Fore was a crooked silhouette, like broken glass, or a lethal, sabre-edged reef jutting out of the water.

"What the devil is that?" Ivor knocked out his pipe on the rail, the better to focus on the danger ahead.

"A mirage?" I hoped.

"There's a chap."

I joined Ivor in leaning forward over the rail and squinted into the almost complete absence of contrast between sky and land and sea. But, indeed, there was a small figure, dancing about.

"I think he's trying to attract our attention," said Ivor.

"Ahoy, reef!" I called. "Could you move out of the way?"

If the little grey figure shouted something back it was lost on the wind.

"What's he doing?" wondered Ivor.

"Signalling, it looks like," came the voice of authority. The captain had arrived on the bow and he'd had the presence of mind or lifelong habit to bring his telescope. He pointed it at the little island. "He has a boat. Two-rigger yawl, looks like. He's boarding her. Probably fetching his flags. Mister Moy! Bring our semaphores, if you please."

But the man on the boat moored at Scary Island didn't want to signal us. In the next instant, a burst of fire lit up the water before him, followed by a chute of smoke, and finally the boom of the cannon reached our ears.

"Hard to port, Mister Moy!" ordered the captain. The engines roared and *The Ballast* listed sharply to starboard. "General quarters, gentlemen — we're under fire."

❦

"Probably no more than an eighteen-pounder," estimated Captain Slapton. "We're out of range."

Dashed remarkable things, telescopes. From where I was standing on the bridge with the captain, the inspector, the first mate, the peer, and the parrot, Scary Island and its sole inhabitant were an indistinguishable slip of horizon. Through the captain's telescope, though, it bloomed into a rich landscape of barren rock, scrub brush, crashing waves on a hostile coast of shards and sharps, and a man on a boat with a cannon pointed at us.

Hold it the other way round, and a telescope makes Inspector Wittersham look as though he's standing at the far end of an immense tunnel, frowning at me.

"Prosperity Skerry." Slapton pointed with his telescope at a chart on a table which, judging by the slipping stack of graphs and maps, was the chart table.

A maritime chart is quite a different thing to, say, a map of the London tube. There are longitudinal and latitudinal lines, soundings, currents, and, of course and in particular on this part of the Scilly Archipelago, countless shoals and atolls and skerries and reefs. From the surface, the sea looks bottomless and safe to sail blindfolded. However, if one goes by the chart, which I understand is widely recommended, it's a labyrinth of razor rocks and cross-currents, navigable only by strict adherence to a narrow and twisting and invisible path.

Prosperity Skerry was no welcome exception. It was a fish-shaped outcropping with rocky tendrils reaching out on all sides, making the place dashed easy and dashed pointless to defend. The island had a great hump in the middle, like a whale or a camel or an island with a great hump in the middle, and as we traced the periphery one could see through the telescope what looked to have once been stone constructions of a certain age.

"There be one safe mooring." Slapton tapped the chart with his telescope, indicating one of the seemingly identical coves formed of natural cays. "And there be a cannon."

"We'll keep the ship out of range," proposed Ivor, "and Minty and I can row ashore."

"Excellent idea," endorsed Lord Archie.

"Minty votes no," dissented Minty.

"We'll fly a flag of truce," said Ivor. "He won't fire on a Scotland Yard inspector flying a flag of truce."

"It's not the cannon that's my chief discern, even if it certainly would be if there weren't no storm." Minty gestured, with a broad, encompassing wave, at everything. Indeed, beyond the bridge and only just outside a small radius on all sides of the yacht, was a rolling, folding wall of pother and gloom, a swirling turmoil the colour of anger rising from the sea to the heavens.

"Ah," agreed Ivor.

"Minty's right," weighted the captain. "There'll be no quarter given jollies, wherries or skiffs once the eye of the storm closes, and she's closing fast."

"Do we just anchor where we are, then, and wait it out?" asked Ivor, thankfully, before I could.

"Don't be daft," advised Slapton. "We'd be dashed on a reef or swallowed whole by a whirlpool. Mister Moy, reverse engines at full, if you please, and be smart about it, then full about and hard for'rd."

"Aye aye, Captain." Minty opened the door and the whistle of wind became a shout, and it whisked the first mate out of sight and slammed the door for him.

"We'll make for Keelover Cove." Slapton leaned over his chart and indicated a nearby blob. "The nearest safe haven, here, on Squall Atoll."

"Is that not where you once capsized, Captain?" I asked, more from idle curiosity than undiluted panic.

"Aye, and it's our only hope," augured Slapton, as the storm closed around us, and swallowed Prosperity Skerry and the entire world.

CHAPTER TWELVE

All the World's a Wager, and All the Men and Women Merely Punters

The engines slowed to a chugging adagio that soon slipped beneath the shrieking allegro of the storm. I was on the port bow and Ivor was starboard, and we acted as parking guides as Captain Slapton in the wheelhouse inched us between dinosaur tooth stalagmites that defined the jaws of the snug haven where he proposed we wait out the weather.

Despite or, possibly, thanks to my frantic waves and warnings, we managed on several occasions to find something with which to scrape the hull with a prolonged vibrato in the key of fear major. As we bumped home I made note of the fact that, if necessary, one could rock-hop ashore and live out one's life on this storm-swept shoal.

Great granite pillars rose from the water around us and put some psychological distance and detachment between us and the howling tempest. Minty moored us to some of the columns and laid on a barrier of rubber bumpers, and a sort of serene siege sensation settled on *The Ballast*. We were still surrounded by swirling fog and a singing wind and waves that played on the boat like a cork on a kettle drum, but we were snug and safe in our little hidy haven.

"I'll look in on you later, if I might, Mister Boisjoly," Ivor announced with the early warnings of a hoarse anguish as he passed on the way to the main deck. "I'll be very much obliged for another jar of seasick medicine."

"Right oh, Inspector," I bluffed. "I'll have Vickers sort you out an economy-sized pot."

I gave him a head start and then made for my own cabin with the clear and unmoveable priority of conjuring up a new batch of seasick elixir, when…

"What ho, Anty."

"Oh, what ho, Teddy." I stopped at Teddy's cabin door, which was open, such that I could see that she was accompanied by a bottle of brandy and an absence of Winnifreds.

"Fancy a snooter? You look as though you could stand one." Teddy held up her snifter and gave it a suggestive swirl, and what with her maritime-motif trousers and topping in navy and white, she looked like she was rehearsing something by Noel Coward.

"You read me like a thirsty book, favourite cousin." I wandered into her cabin and discarded the dripping pea coat, under which I was happily and habitually dressed for cocktails. "Tie one directly on."

"What's going on out there?" Teddy handed over a round round one. "Sounds like the dragons are winning."

"Well, we arrived at Prosperity Skerry," I reported. "But it appears that the only inhabitant has a fixed prejudice against postmen. And a cannon."

"I heard that from Mints, but he had little time for details."

"He was on his way to the engine room to effect a retreat. I don't know how long it takes to reload an eighteen-pounder, but I think it's reasonable to say that time was pressing." I inhaled a savoury snout of artisanal French heritage. "Since then we've taken refuge at another island."

"Is there a casino?"

"No, but where it lacks in basic amenities it has an abundance of razor rock and wind." I sipped my brandy for a pensive moment. "I say, Teds, are you all right, and all that?"

"I'm simply tinkly, Ants, why do you ask?"

"I mean to say, what with Dare indefinitely cancelling the milk."

"What do you mean?" asked Teddy over her snifter. "Has something happened to Dare?"

"Oh my giddy aunt's guinea stamp," I rued. "I thought you knew."

"Of course I knew, Anty." Teddy beamed the very smile I first saw when I learned that, contrary to her assurances, Nanny O'Malley was not a Russian Tsarina. "We're on a boat, and there are ten of us. In any case, I had the inspector asking me where I was all day."

"So you're alright then?"

"I am. It's a terrible thing, of course. He was a nice chap and I'm sure he loved his mother, but we weren't a sensation, if that's what you're thinking. He hadn't even asked me to marry him."

"Don't most chaps get 'round to that straight after introductions?"

"As a rule." Teddy nodded. "Clearly, it wasn't meant to be. Made for a dashed convenient disqualifier, I'll confess. Bunny and Caspar looked like rival cricket captains trying to get a fox off the pitch."

"And there aren't a lot of foxes that'll let you ride on their backs."

"I twisted my ankle," persisted Teddy.

"No, you didn't."

"No, I didn't." Teddy looked to her brandy for understanding. "They wanted me to run, Anty. Claimed we were late getting back to the boat."

"So I heard. And then you all went to Dare's cabin for brandy."

"Not all," recalled Teddy with a glance at the ceiling. "Caspar demurred."

"Curious," I called it. "He said that he was there."

"Oh, he was there, he just didn't drink anything." Teddy referred once again to the ceiling for confirmation. "It struck me as odd, as though he didn't want to accept Dare's largesse. He was quite standoffish, to put a word to it."

"Bunny drank, though."

"Oh boy, yes."

"And you saw none of them since," I said, and casually snifted my snifter.

"I saw Freddy. Does Freddy count?"

"She does," I said. "You know that Freddy isn't Freddy, don't you?"

"Of course she is," differed Teddy. "Who else do you think she is?"

"I mean to say that the Freddy I was expecting was Frederica Hannibal-Pool."

"You don't mean that."

"I most seriously, torturously, do."

"You thought the Freddy that was joining this trip was Frederica," said Teddy with an awed, slightly to mightily mocking tone. The sort of tone one takes when a chap says he's invested in a scheme to move the Eiffel Tower to Brighton.

"Why else did you think I wanted to come along on the voyage?"

"To support your favourite cousin in her time of need," lectured Teddy. "At least, that's what you told me."

"And that's still very much the case," I claimed. "But you see, I've been writing to Freddy."

"Which Freddy?"

"The wrong Freddy, it turns out."

"You must absolutely be making that up," revelled Teddy. "This is the very frozen limit. You've been writing all those letters to Winnie? Didn't you ever twig?"

"Of course I twigged," I corrected with cool pride. "Today, when I saw her."

"But, Anty, they're entirely separate people," pointed out Teddy. "Frederica's a tall glass of fizz on a toot on the town with a hundred quid and a false name, and Winnifred is… not that."

"I thought that she was demonstrating a ladylike reserve."

"Freddy?" marvelled Teddy. "The same Freddy who hijacked a horse costume at the Richmond Theatre panto, just so she could kick George Jackley in front of a live audience?"

"Exactly," I said. "And most definitively not the Freddy who walked out of the panto at the Palladium when she got confetti in her hair."

"Not that Freddy, no."

"Did ur-Freddy really dress as a horse and kick George Jackley at the Richmond Theatre?"

"No, not really," admitted Teddy. "That was me. Freddy was the front end, though."

"Excellent venue for infiltrating panto dressed as a horse, the Richmond."

"Second only to the Lyceum," agreed Teddy. "Tell you what Freddy did do... let's agree to call them Freddy and Winnie, shall we?"

"Or Freddy and Winds of Whinge," I offered, with an amenable tilt of my glass. "I'm fine either way."

"I'll tell you what Freddy did do, she only nobbled a West End play for fun and profit."

"Is that something one does?"

"It's something one does if one has a bookie threatening to have an open and frank discussion with one's papa," tipped Teddy. "It seems Freddy heard about this caper, known only to the tightest insiders, the wheeze of which is that rare and certain musical comedies on rare and certain nights were going to throw the match, as it were."

"Not really."

"Turns out, no, not really," recounted Teddy. "It was someone's idea of a flying great lark to tell Freddy that a Friday night sellout of *Funny Face* was going to change the ending, and instead of a song-and-dance number and a wedding, the finale was going to be a bloodbath."

"She didn't believe that," I doubted. "Not Freddy."

"Apparently her source was very convincing."

"But, *Funny Face,*" I continued along doubting lines. "It's got Fred Astaire in it."

"That's what drove up the odds," explained Teddy. "For one night only, the entire third act was going to be lifted whole from *Sweeney Todd.* Astaire was going to run amok with, first, a straight razor, then a scythe."

"I hope Freddy didn't overextend herself."

"She pledged her father's membership of The Jockey Club as security against a stake of a hundred pounds."

"Daring," I observed. "One of the greatest of her father's simple joys is voting down American turf rules."

"And obviously she had no difficulty finding a bookie prepared to offer long odds that Fred Astaire wasn't going to play an axe murderer," said Teddy. "And even more obviously she lost the bet, hence the bookie with the life-altering appointment with Freddy's father."

"So when does all this nobbling come in?" I wanted to know.

"One week later, at a showing of *Ooh-La-La* at The Shaftesbury." Teddy finished her brandy and squeezed the last of the bottle into her glass. "She had to get back on the black side of the ledger, so she doubled down. She offered the same tout even odds that the Saturday showing of *Ooh-La-La* was going to swap out its big finale and instead of ending with a Can-Can they were going to make the audience stand for *God Save The King.*"

"*Ooh-La-La?*" I rationed myself a sip of brandy. "Didn't that close earlier this year under protest by the League for Public Decency?"

"That's the one."

"I saw it," I confessed. "Very coquettish and fish-nettish. She convinced a bookie that *Ooh-La-La* was going to drop its big, leggy finish in favour of the national anthem?"

"No, she convinced a bookie that she believed it, and he took her bet."

"Doubtless with a song in his heart."

"Doubtless," agreed Teddy. "But then, on the night of the performance in question, just before the big finale, the stage director received a cable saying that the king had died, owing to a combination of septicaemia, pneumonia, and falling face-first out of a taxi."

"Credible."

"The band played *God Save the King* in honour of Edward VIII, our new king," Teddy drank to the memory of George V, "and they lowered the curtain."

"You sent the cable, I take it."

"I did."

"So, it was you, not Freddy, who nobbled a West End show for fun and profit."

"No, just for fun," differed Teddy. "And for a friend. Otherwise it would have been unethical. In any case, it was the least I could do — it was me who told Freddy that Fred Astaire was going to go on a murder spree."

"I assumed as much." Taking a strongly preservationist position on brandy, I merely observed my glass longingly. "Any idea why?"

"It was the only way I could get her to go with me," claimed Teddy. "My escort for the evening was Bash Postcode, or whatever his name is."

"Postcombe."

"That's it." Teddy toasted my powers of recollection with the last of the brandy. "Nice enough chap, but boring as flooring. I needed someone to talk to. You can understand that."

"Of course."

"So, all is forgiven then, is it?"

"Retroactively and in advance, Tedds," I assured her, "but it's not me decides these things. You'll probably want to sketch out these thoughts in a letter to the editor of *The Times* theatre section."

"Not the West End jape — that's just business as usual. No, I mean to say... don't you know... well, Bash and Freddy rather hit it off."

"Hit what off?"

"It," specified Teddy. "He really rather emerged from the shell, did young Bash. Did you know that he's a member of the Royal Society?"

"I did not."

"He is. Special expertise in snails or turtles or some such. He's going to name a species after Freddy."

"You don't say."

"Oh, and they're engaged," said Teddy. "You're not miffed, are you, Ants?"

"No."

"You've still got Winnifred."

"Yes, on consideration, I'm miffed," I amended. "Vexed, even. And forgiveness withdrawn. It was you who gave me the address of the wrong Freddy."

"You should have been more specific," said Teddy. "They sound quite similar, Freddy and Freddy, you'll admit. How bad were the letters?"

"There may have been poetry," I mourned.

"You think you're going to have to marry her?"

"No. Her parents would never have me."

"Are you mad?" scoffed Teddy. "They love you. Always have. Ever since you came into your father's money."

I looked to the portal windows, which the whirlwind was now whipping with water and weeds. The storm sang a singular song of

115

the surging sea, and the boat rolled rhythmically and the hull thumped and bumped the walls of our little cove.

"Perhaps we'll sink," I yearned, and emptied my glass for the third time.

"If you want more brandy, Anty, just say so."

"Is there more brandy?" I gazed meaningfully at the bottle that she had defeated almost single-handedly.

"One way to find out — I got this one from Dare. There's probably more in his stateroom."

"When did you acquire a bottle from Dare's stateroom?"

"He gave it to me, if memory serves," Teddy once again referred to the ceiling, "when we went our separate ways this afternoon."

"He didn't come here, then, to this cabin."

"Well, of course not, Anthony Boisjoly," protested Teddy. "What makes you say such a thing?"

"Just speculating," I piffled. "I was wondering if he gave you the bottle at the same time that he gave you that map you have hanging on the wall."

Teddy looked at the wall behind her.

"What map?"

"The only map on the wall, Teddy," I reduced for clarity. "The only map on any wall on this entire ship — all the other pictures are depictions of naval battles."

"Yes, very well, Anty, Dare gave it to me," admitted Teddy. "He thought it was safer hidden in plain sight in my room rather than hidden the old-fashioned way in his."

I examined the map. It recalled, in a rough, hand-hewn way, the chart that I'd seen on the bridge. There were three little blobs, the largest of which was Prosperity Skerry, with Squall Atoll and Sneaky Reef labelled on either side, longitudinally speaking. Sneaky Reef had no other markings and Squall Atoll had only Keelover Cove, Brokestone Bay, Viking Fire Pit, and Roman Graveyard. Prosperity

Skerry, by contrast, was a lost civilisation of coves and lagoons surrounding its own Roman Graveyard, a Viking village, a hill called Pilyek Pile, and a rainwater well. It also had a big red X on it, very much in keeping with the pirate map aesthetic.

"No," preempted Teddy. "That's not the location of the treasure. Apparently the X just indicates the island. The other map gives the precise location."

"So I understand," I said. "What's the point of entrusting it to you, though? We all know that the island under discussion is Prosperity Skerry. Without the other map this one is almost common knowledge."

"Probably he just wanted to keep them separate," suggested Teddy.

"Keep what separate?" I wondered. "Caspar told me that Dare only had the one map."

"That's what he told Caspar. Clearly it was what he wanted to hear, but Dare had both maps."

CHAPTER THIRTEEN

Of Snitches and Riches and Infinite Ipswiches

The sea twitched and the boat pitched and I biffed the door across the corridor. Then the sea rolled to and the boat did too and I reeled back into Teddy's cabin. I followed the next wave back into action and took hold of the handle.

"Good evening, sir."

Vickers, who has the sea legs of an elastic octopus, was in tempo with the corridor, as was the perfectly balanced tray in his hand.

"What ho, Vickers," I swayed.

"First Mate Moy has proposed that we dine in our cabins this evening, sir, owing to the inclement weather and his advanced state of inebriation."

"Right oh," I acceded. "I'm not fussy. Bit of sole meunière and chips seems to fit the occasion."

"I regret, sir…"

"No, I know, I'll have the usual ration of hard biscuit and pork risk-it."

The deck reeled to starboard and Teddy skidded on stage.

"What ho, Vickers."

"Good evening, Miss Quillfeather. I have brought biscuits and preserved pork matter."

"Mmmm. Hope you brought plenty to go round," said Teddy. "It's okay, everything goes better with brandy. Brandy goes better with brandy. Have you got the key to this door, Vickers?"

"Yes, Miss — First Mate Moy provided me with the master key." Vickers produced said master key. "I shall place the… tray in your stateroom, sir."

"Thank you, Vickers." I received the key and, after a bit of to-ing and fro-ing and then a bit more fro-ing, unlocked Dare's door. "Oh, and if you would, stir up another jar of that seasick medicine that we gave to Inspector Wittersham."

"Seasick medicine, sir?"

"Well, no, not really seasick medicine." I lowered my tone to conspiracy volume. "You know, that fixer elixir we mixed up in your marmalade jar."

"Oh, yes, sir," twigged Vickers. "If you would refresh my memory with respect to the ingredients."

"You don't remember either?"

"I fear not."

"No matter," I offhanded. "Just mix a bit of grog and equal parts shandy. and brandy in a marmalade pot and deliver it to the inspector with due gravitas and my compliments."

"Very good, sir."

An eerie blue gloom flowed through Dare's room until I found the desk lamp on the liquor cabinet. Now an eerie yellow joined the eerie blue to form an eerie aqua, glooming and glimmering like spirits on the ceiling, jostled and harried by the storm. The ceiling spirits were accompanied by what sounded like a full-throated hurricane by this time, whipping and whistling through the rigging and the pillars that walled our little port. It was all outside, though, beyond a heavy hull in which we were cradled and rocked, and indeed it was the very violence of the tempest only feet away that made the dim, warm refuge feel that much more like an attic library on a rainy day.

"Oh, ho!" Teddy raised a triumphant bottle from the liquor cabinet.

"Oh, ho ho!" I raised the cigar box from the top of same.

"Dare's treasure box," spotted Teddy. "I wonder the inspector hasn't taken charge of it."

"I expect he thought it was safest here," I speculated. "He wouldn't know the master key yacht trivia, and in any case we already determined that the map was gone. We didn't know you had it, of course."

"I wonder what's become of the other." Teddy gave voice to the elephant in the room while carefully weighing the brandy v soda question.

."Presumably the killer has it." I opened the cigar box on the divan. "It's obviously the more valuable of the two, as it shows where on the island the treasure is buried."

"Doubtless you're right." Teddy handed me my 'tizer. "Anty, what do you suppose your place in Kensington is worth?"

"The house in Kensington?" I puzzled. "In order of interest — why do you ask? And I have no idea."

"Lord Archie has a similar sort of shack, hasn't he?"

"He has," I said. "The Hannibal-Pools are much closer to the palace, but I'm much further from the Hannibal-Pools, so very comparable in terms of property values. Are you thinking of giving up the flat in Chelsea?"

"I might be…" Teddy sipped meditatively. "Will you ask Lord Archie what he thinks a place like yours could be had for? I understand he has something of an eye for a bargain."

"I'll ask him if you like, but I would characterise His Lordship's gift more as a flair for the false economy," I said. "In addition to countless boondoggles, including a billiards table installed on this very boat, he owns a Shetland vineyard and a stud farm for rabbits, both of which he acquired at giveaway prices."

"At least he'll have some idea of the value of his own property, Anty."

"Well, then, why don't you ask him yourself?" I suggested. "I get tremendously anxious discussing money and the like with chaps. It's the same feeling I get when I'm chatting with a vicar and he mentions the Sermon on the Mount, or any conversation between two or more blokes which inevitably turns to the subject of motorcars, their care in sickness and in health."

"I understand, Anty, but Lord Archie knows my father."

"So do I know your father," I said, neatly making my counterpoint. "He's my uncle."

"Yes, but you wouldn't tell Papa that I'm pricing houses in Kensington," parried Teddy. "Lord Archie most absolutely would."

"That's true, he would. I recall he couldn't wait to tell my father when I got pinched for a lock-in party at the Coach and Horses."

"There you go."

"As it happened, my father already knew," I said. "He was on the docket right after me at Bow Street Magistrates', having been pinched for a lock-in party at the Buckingham. So, no real harm done, but it shows Lord Archie had and has the snitch's spirit."

"So, you'll ask him?"

"Very well, cryptic cousin," I conceded, "but, forgive my curiosity if it's misplaced, if your father's to be kept in the dark about your empire-building ambitions in Kensington, how do you propose to finance them?"

"The Cambridge Festival Theatre is doing *Romeo and Juliet* this summer," mused Teddy. "I'm thinking of backing odds on a happy ending."

"I must get tickets early." I idly shuffled about in the cigar box. "I say, Tedds, you're quite sure that Dare said that he had both maps."

"Quite sure."

"And equally sure that he didn't give you both of them."

"Just the one, Anty," said Teddy. "I counted it twice, to be absolutely sure."

I did a cigar box inventory — the journal, a list of names and ranks, suggestive of a ship's crew, and a finely detailed accounting of the freight of three vessels, including '*5000 gouden dukaten*' that had been in the hold of Dutch East Indies Company ship, *Vergulde Kip.*

Meanwhile, Teddy teetered across Dare's reception room in time with the waves, examining the paintings and analysing the brandy.

"Possibly the second map is still here, somewhere." Teddy swayed before an immense, all-burning, all-smoking, all-sinking depiction of the Battle of Trafalgar. "Maybe Dare hid it in plain view, like he did the first one."

"Caspar's case that there's no second map rests on the improbability of the entire story." As one does when one excises a journal from a cigar box, I was flipping pages randomly and fell upon the account of the last hours of John Mucknell's ship, *The John.* "According to this unattributed account, *The John* was heading home after an exhausting business trip, laden with golden ducats and other such souvenirs, when it was confronted by three ships of the line; The *Constant Warwick, The Expedition,* and *The Cygnet.* Caspar finds it unlikely that *The John* could have fought the enemy to a standstill and made her escape yet still need to offload its treasure to a sister ship — called *The Phoenix* — only to stay above sea level long enough to run aground."

"It does rather test the bounds, doesn't it?" judged Teddy. "I mean to say, 'Constant Warwick'? Not 'Infinite Ipswich' or 'Good Ol' Bognor Regis'?"

"I think it was less the names of the ships and more the circumstances of the battle with which Caspar took issue," I clarified.

"He missed a trick then," said Teddy. "But yes, he said as much this afternoon."

"Ah, but did he also say that there was no such boat as *The Phoenix?*"

"He did," said Teddy. "And he would brook no dissent."

"So Dare didn't dispute it."

"No. In fact he appeared to agree with Caspar."

"And yet, right here in this journal is the history of a ship called, at various times in its colourful career, *The Phoenix, The Excellent,* His Majesty's Prison Ship *Decadent,* and then again *The Phoenix.* Launched in 1613, she saw action in Ireland and was reputedly scrapped in 1624 as its timbers were needed to build a gallows, a pier, and a tea room in Dingle. But the ship never arrived in Dingle. It was rechristened again and then again and then won, by a certain Roger Smalley, in a game of 'Stab'. Smalley recognised *The Phoenix,* having served on her as first mate for several years with a general mandate to spread ill-will against England from Dunmore to Cork."

"Smalley was the Captain Clever who made off with the plunder from *The John,* promising to return it later," toasted Teddy.

"That's the chap." I flipped back a page or two to something else that had caught my eye. "There's an account here from the perspective of the signalman on *The John.*" I read the following passage to Teddy…

The captaine gave orders that The Phoenix *shouldst join the battle. The signale was flagged up, but came no replye for somme tyme, during which* The John *exchanged another broadside with* Constant Warwick, *costing us, in order of prioritye, two guns, a jolly boat, a barrel of powder, the ship ferret, and three men.*

In tyme, The Phoenix *did signalle that she was sorry she hadst seen not our flagging, as she had been watching the sunset. Again the signal was made that* The Phoenix *should join the fraye, and* The Phoenix *replied that she would do so, but she was short of powder and the will to sink for a lost cause.*

Captaine Mucknell ordered that The Phoenix *be signalled she could join the battle or, at earlyest convenience, Captaine Smalley shouldst find a moment for Captain Mucknell to chop his ears off.*

For somme goode tyme Captain Mucknell was occupyed with the parlyament shippes, which did vexe The John *with cannon fire at our water line, and the captain ordered that our gunners should sweepe the deck of the rebel ships with a view to demasting them.*

When the gunnes did finally quiet, the parlyament ships were bestill'd and The John *was sinking and I commended my soul to heaven or my body to the parlyament shippes, which I beleaved were getting the better of two bads.*

The captaine ordered a course back to Scilly by way of France and so it was we were fayre up to our gunwales and there was a portypuss in the galley afore we sighted lande. Captaine Mucknell, it was said, planned to run us aground on Saint Mary's but with the tide low and the hold busting with gold we made to lighten the ship. We jettisoned the cannons and anchor and the keele was stille scraping the reefes, so when The Phoenix *showed herself and signalled do we neede assistance the captaine bid me answere a lengthy message that I durst not repeate here, and with tyme so shorte and not wishing to be drowndead in sight of lande, I signalled only 'yes'.*

So it was that the golde was shifted to the hold of The Phoenix, *but then in steade of escorting us to ground she beat about and did tack due northe by east. Captain Mucknell ordered a sweep of her rigging, and our gunnes cracked her rear yard, such that she was obliged to about and sail ahead of a southerly wind.*

The Phoenix *was gone and so was all the golde we tooke fayre and square off two English shippes and a Duch, but* The John *was light enough now to run aground on the sand off Innisidgen.*

"Was it spelt that way or are you working on a character?" asked Teddy.

"I feel it added a certain rustic authenticity."

"You sounded like Minty reading a letter to his nan, the pirate," said Teddy. "I see your point, though — it holds up. *The Phoenix* was running off with the treasure but lost a mast or two and had to put in at the nearest island where Mucknell wouldn't find them. They hid the treasure on Prosperity Skerry so they wouldn't have it on them while sailing jury-rigged and vulnerable, and they hobbled back to England."

The storm expressed itself now in an insistent, urgent soprano, rather like The Queen of the Night aria from *The Magic Flute,* performed by a coloratura soprano being pursued by Fred Astaire with a straight razor. The boat was no longer rocking as it was undulating. It seemed to be moving on both axes plus a new one it had invented for itself, as though we were being tossed by the seas and the seas, in turn, were riding the Chatham milk train.

Teddy mixed two more bubbly brandies and joined me on the divan. She took an idle, something-to-do-while-sipping-brandy interest in the peripheral documents.

"Dare performed this for us last night. I don't know how official it is, but this account certainly backs up the theory." Teddy leaned back with a crisp, yellowed sheet of ephemera. "Listen to this…

A ship so battle-worn and calloused
With a draught up to her gunwales
She sailed for home with gold for ballast
And ribbons where were once sails

When three barks of the commonwealth
On course for the isles of the outer seas
Barred her from her home and help
She tacked a course towards all three

A thousand times she ran out her guns
As The Phoenix watched the fires dim
Then signalled 'stay, we've just begun'
And she trimmed her mizzen in

Then she quit the fire and smoke still settling
By wind, by fortune, and by dead reckoning

But as sea rushed in at either side
She picked her passage through the shoals
She hobbled home and there she died
And finally loosed her cursed load

Within sight of Saint Mary's lee
Where the gathered pool is calm
She finally slip't beneath the sea
Where ancient sailors meet their gods

Her final act to disgorge her gold
The riches that low cunning made
Into the pirate traitor's hold
From then on that's where they stayed

Where did The Phoenix finally go?
To her nest on the isle of Prospero

"Curious," I commented. "But I'm not sure how it advances the investigation. Whoever wrote it obviously knew that *The Phoenix* had gone to Prosperity Skerry, but he might have just seen the map or maps."

"Okay, then, how about this…" Teddy picked up the presumed crew list. "Captain… Roger Smalley."

"This would be the crew of *The Phoenix,* then."

"I almost hope not, Anty." Teddy assumed a grave tone. "Have a look at the first mate."

The very next entry, in fact, after 'Captain... Roger Smalley' was 'First Mate... Sam Starbuck'."

CHAPTER FOURTEEN

The Vices and Vulnerabilities of a Vickers in Vigor

"Inspector Wittersham wishes me to convey his strong desire to see you at your earliest convenience, sir."

Vickers was in the stateroom, doing something stately with the room.

"He doesn't know the half of it, Vickers," I said. "There have been developments in the case."

"Miss Hannibal-Pool also expressed her desire for an interview," added Vickers in a distracted tone as he puzzled over the far greater mystery of the presence of duplicate school ties.

"Did you tell her I had gone to the countryside?"

"The artifice, I felt, would have lacked verisimilitude."

"No, that's probably true. Did she say what she wanted?"

"She expressed surprise that you had not yet found it convenient to offer her comfort and sympathy, sir, in light of the cannon fire, the storm, and other such adversity under which she is currently labouring."

"Yes, poor leaf, she must be feeling quite persecuted."

"This is very much the impression she conveyed," agreed Vickers.

"Right oh, I'll just put on something dryer, have a long reconnoitre with Scotland Yard, and grow a beard," I said. "Please tell Miss Hannibal-Pool that I'll see her sometime in the new year, if you can't avoid her."

Always scornful of Cleopatra's advice to let ill tidings tell themselves, Vickers fired the other barrel, "I should inform you that His Lordship and Her Ladyship are also anxious for an audience."

"I'll just bet they are," I wagered. "Have you ever been sued for breach of promise, Vickers?"

"Yes, sir."

"Really?"

"Yes, sir." Vickers set aside the duplicate tie question until the morning light brought the clarity that duplicate ties can wait till morning. "I briefly had an understanding with a Miss Irene Codicote, the upstairs maid of Lord Fern-Spackler's Chelsea address."

"The Fern-Spacklers don't live in Chelsea," I pointed out.

"This was not the late Lord Fern-Spackler, sir, but his grandfather."

"So, going back a bit."

"This would have been January of 1870."

"What's the procedure, then?" I asked. "There's some sort of financial settlement, presumably, and a bit of ostracisation? These days I expect it's a stinging pun in the society pages — something like 'Bandy Boisjoly' — but back then I assume one was tarred and feathered. Does the tar stay long in one's hair, Vickers?"

"Miss Codicote demanded a settlement of one hundred pounds."

"A hundred quid?" I staggered. "In 1870? With a hundred pounds in 1870 you could buy Canada."

"I expect the amount of the settlement was commensurate with the Boisjoly fortune, and she had an iron-clad case," admitted Vickers. "There were letters."

"Letters, you say."

"I'm afraid so. And poetry."

"Poetry?" I disdained. "Really, Vickers."

"She was a most attractive young lady," offered Vickers in his defence. "And I had only met her while we were both on duty."

"Presumably the scales fell from your eyes."

"During a shooting weekend at the Berkshire estate." Vickers nodded dully into a traumatised past. "She displayed a tendency to snort when she laughed, and to laugh frequently, and often at the most inscrutable things, such as a candle burning out quite expectedly, or turnips."

"But by then you'd already committed the commitment of comitant youth to pen and paper," I surmised.

"In a most legally-binding fashion," agreed Vickers.

"Did my grandfather really stump up a hundred pounds?"

"It was his father, your great-grandfather, who eventually negotiated the settlement." Vickers set about assembling tonight's tweeds and tie. "He invited the household for another shooting weekend, to provide Miss Codicote opportunity to familiarise herself with her new life as my wife and a member of the Boisjoly domestic staff. Then he left for the continent, giving your grandfather full run of the estate as host."

"Ah."

"Yes, sir." Vickers positioned the tweed trousers for takeoff. "She remained steadfastly affiancéed through the horses in the dining room and even the flooding of the gatehouse, but by the time the weekend was over she pronounced herself lucky to get out with ten pounds and her sanity. I don't believe there was any one single breaking point, but she was particularly unnerved when she saw the footprints on the ceiling of the games room, at which point she offered me five pounds to discreetly call off the wedding."

"Probably not a very practical strategy in the current circumstances." I stepped between current and future trousers. "The Hannibal-Pools are already quite familiar with the Boisjoly reputation for ceiling footprints. What do you suppose it would cost to buy Canada today?"

"I doubt very much that Miss Hannibal-Pool would be satisfied with that which would content an upstairs maid."

"Speaking as someone close to the subject, Vickers, I can confirm that Miss Hannibal-Pool wouldn't be satisfied with twice and a half that which would content the Aga Khan." I reversed deftly into the proffered waistcoat. "Should she come calling, tell her that I'm in conference with the inspector, and that I'm expected to be some time, and she should return to her stateroom and start a new life."

"I fear it will be nearly impossible to avoid the Hannibal-Pools indefinitely on board this ship," doomspake Vickers.

"And yet, that's just what I'm going to do," I assured him. "I shall avoid Lord and Lady Hannibal-Pool almost as assiduously as I shall their daughter. I shall be a shadow, a wisp, I shall ride on a moonbeam and hide in a jacket seam. We may need to switch rooms. Does yours have a sturdy lock?"

I torsoed the tweed jacket and sent Vickers on ahead to scout out the terrain.

"The corridor is empty, sir."

"Then I'm off across the hall — that's for your ears only, if it need be said."

I caught the next roll of the sea and skidded downhill into Ivor's door.

"Come in…" Ivor's uneven delivery boded ill and dizzy. I went in.

The room was dark and made darker by closed curtains and the mysterious, delirious lump of inspector sitting on the bed, hugging an ice bucket.

"What ho, Inspector," I stage whispered. "Anything the matter?"

"Immunity…" croaked Ivor. "I've developed an immunity to the seasick remedy."

"Nonsense." I felt the best approach, in the absence of any other ideas at all, was stout denial. "There's no such thing as immunity to the seasick remedy. It has a uniform effect on all people, like basset puppies."

Ivor appeared to want to shake his head, and even made a game attempt at getting a bit of it to the left, but then thought the better of it.

"No. You said that if it doesn't taste of rum, pork brine, orange zest, and lime, it means I'm immune."

"I said that?" I asked, I confess, disingenuously, for as quickly as Ivor recounted it I recalled it. "I think you might be misremembering. Have a bit more."

"I've had the lot." Ivor's head pitched back with the roll of the ship, biffed the wall behind him, and then dropped forward again, like a rag doll losing hope. "If anything it's making me feel worse. Tastes and feels like brandy and grog."

"Ah, I know what's happened," which was, indisputably, the truth. "Vickers must have got the recipe confused with the Boisjoly family remedy for handmaid's knee. You don't have handmaid's knee, do you Inspector?"

"No."

"Well, there you go then." I collected the marmalade pot and weaved delicately and circuitously in a doorly direction.

"Just a minute…" Ivor invested a great deal into that, and required a moment of moaning before he could continue. "If I can't go on… you have to take up the investigation. It mustn't wait till we're back on the mainland."

"I daresay you're right, Inspector," I agreed. "I may have discovered a most intriguing insight among the crew list of *The Phoenix.*"

"First Mate Sam Starbuck."

"The very one," I said. "Also, there may be good cause to believe that Dare had both maps."

"Maps…"

"Treasure maps, Inspector, the likely motive for the murder."

"Murder..." Ivor's voice tripped dreamily over the word, as though it reminded him of Christmas as a boy.

"The first map is hanging on the wall of Teddy's stateroom," I reported.

"Teddy... bear?"

"My cousin Theodora," I clarified. "Dare gave her the map indicating Prosperity Skerry."

"You have a lot of cousins, Anty."

"I do... what did you call me?"

"Far too many, for just one chap, if you ask me." Ivor's head lolled and his eyes appeared to be operating independently. "You toffs, always getting more than your share of everything."

"We're not so very different, we toffs, Inspector," I calmly countered, "we put our jodhpurs on one leg at a time, just like anyone else."

"You don't have to tell me, Anty Boisjoly..." Ivor spoke a sort of sloshing summation, like a barrister defending himself in court against a charge of being drunk in court. "I know you. I know just your measure."

"Steady on, Inspector, you don't want to say something that later turns out to be true."

"You..." Ivor hugged his ice bucket like a long-lost stuffed aardvark. "You're a good chap, Anty."

"How dare you sir."

"And you're a friend." Ivor tried to look me square in the eye but caught me somewhere about shoulder height. "I don't have many friends, Anty, that's how I know."

It's dashed difficult to retaliate to a dam burster of that magnitude. My only real preparation was once when I was eleven my father told me that he was proud of me, and that was on the occasion on which

133

he encountered me in the servants' hall on return from my school Nativity Play and, still in costume, he thought I'd grown a beard.

I was quickly assembling something safely Shakespearean, along the lines of 'Words are easy, like the wind; Faithful friends are hard to find', but Ivor wasn't yet done filtering his feelings through the fog of grog and shandy and brandy and mal-de-mer.

"I wouldn't want it to get about I said it, Anty..." Ivor nodded in a curious manner, which is to say he appeared to be curious about whatever it was made him nod, then his head dropped into the ice bucket, such that his next words had all the heartfelt eloquence of a man whispering into an ice bucket. "...but you're a top-flight detective."

"Well, words are easy, like the wind, Inspector..."

"It's all so dashed unjust..." Ivor raised his head from the bucket, but raised it too far, and it biffed the wall again. "Born to an easy life, best of everything without so much as having to say please..."

"They say, don't you know, that words are easy, like the wind..."

"By all rights, you should be the pea-brained waster I thought you were when we first met... and then you turn out to be a sterling bloke."

"...a faithful friend is hard to find."

Outside the elements clashed and crashed and shouted at each other. The wind churned the sea and the waves slapped high into the air and against the hull and windows. *RMS Ballast* dipped its stern and raised its bow and bucked in its close little pen like a wild bull on a sunny day in Spain.

Ivor grimaced at something somewhere in the rough middle distance between us. Whatever it was — the spectre of his old trench sergeant would be my guess — it appeared to inspire him to divine new springs of strength. He set aside the bucket. He positioned both feet as flatly and firmly as one can on a floor that's pitching googlies. He shifted forward, as one intending to rise, but kept right on shifting forward until he was on his knees, then on his hands and knees, and then flat on his face on the floor.

"Boisjoly..." he moaned, returning somewhat to form, "...you'll have to continue the investigation. Talk to everyone — 'specially Lord Habable."

"That will be unnecessary, Inspector, not to mention unnecessarily awkward." I held up the marmalade pot as a beacon of hope. "I'll sort you a new dose of stability tonic and you'll be persecuting the privileged class in the teeth of the most rollicking storm, and enjoying every wobble and sway."

"Nnnnrrrr," replied Ivor, cryptically.

"Be quick about it, you say?"

"No... whatever happens, we must identify the killer before we return to the mainland." Ivor struggled and doubled and snuggled until he was sitting on the floor. He held his face in his hands and pointed it at me. "Or before we set foot on the island — if we go to Prosperity Skerry before finding the second map, there'll be more death to come."

CHAPTER FIFTEEN

The Rime of the Ancient Marinated

"Can you remember this, Vickers?" I said upon return to my stateroom. "Rum grog, pork brine, marmalade and lime."

"No, sir."

"No, quite right," I saw the value in his quick and forthright assessment of the question. "Can you recall where you last saw First Mate Minty Moy?"

"Yes, sir," Vickers said with not undue surprise. "I last saw him in the ship's store, and I fancy he's still there."

"Pickled, is he?"

"To the very roots, sir," confirmed Vickers. "Shall I fetch him for you?"

"No, I'll manage. You stay here and deny you've seen me. Deny you know me, if necessary."

"Very good, sir."

❦

"Ah, Mister Boisjoly." Minty, after what sounded a determined struggle between man and barrel and some sacking, opened the door far enough to peer around it, preceded by a low-pressure warm front of rum.

"What ho, Minters," I greeted. "I have need of something from the ship's store."

"Grog?"

"No, not grog," I said. "Plenty of that in my cabin. What else have you got?"

"Ehm..." Minty closed the door and, judging by the sounds, returned to the battle with renewed but ultimately misplaced hope. The door reopened and the Minty mug reappeared. "Nothing, sir. Just grog."

"Very well. Let's see... I'll have a bottle of cognac, if you please."

"Very good, sir... I mean to say, eh?"

"Come along, Minty, I know as well as you do that this store room is packed to the water line with brandy and, I suspect, tobacco and coffee, all in crates and sacks marked, unimaginatively, 'grog', and all — or at least that which survives the voyage — intended for the discerning market of those who don't like paying import duty."

"Are you insulating that I'm involved in illegal smuggling, Mister Boisjoly?" asked Minty with a wholly failed imitation of hauteur.

"I am," I said. "Not to mention other tautologies, such as misplaced malapropisms and excessive tattoos." I held out my hand. "One bottle of cognac, if you please, Merpins six-year, if you have it, which you do."

Minty looked furtively over my shoulder into the darkness, and then drew back the door. I followed it into the store room, which looked largely as it always did, cluttered with crates and barrels and, as earlier reports indicated, even sacks labelled 'grog'.

"You won't indulge this to anyone, will you, Mister Boisjoly?" Minty pulled away the neck of a sack to reveal a wooden crate stamped 'Merpins'.

"Only the inspector."

"If I could just say a word about that..."

"It's out of my hands, Minty." I held up my hands, conclusively proving the point. "He must be told, but in his current state his reaction is unpredictable. He may arrest you, or he may declare you his best mate. It's not really a toss-up, either — there are plenty of options in between."

"What if I was to jettison the lot?"

"Dump six-year Merpins overboard, Minty?" I gasped aghast. "Then I would not only turn you in, I'd denounce you in the papers."

"They'll send me to prison." Minty handed over the bottle.

"Nonsense," I scorned. "People don't go to prison for smuggling. They pay a fine, or something. Lord Hannibal-Pool's probably responsible for half the grappa consumed in southwest London, and he's never been to prison."

"His Lordship knows the king," pointed out Minty. "People what's don't know the king, in my expedience, and who divulge in a little harmless smuggling, are much more likely to go to prison."

"Yes, I can see how that would follow," I sympathised. "Very well, Minty, tell me this — how did you get the stuff aboard — and I'll try to forget that it's here."

"I can't really say, Mister Boisjoly."

"Because you would be betraying a trust," I surmised. "That of Captain Slapton."

"Please don't tell him I said so, Mister Boisjoly."

"Make it two bottles of brandy," I offered, "and tell me the truth — what were you and Mister Flashburn really discussing this afternoon?"

"Brandy."

"I know," I said. "I deduced that from the fact that yesterday he had only grog to offer his guests, and today he had brandy, and there was sugar for the tea. Dare obviously got the brandy from you — it was to this that you were referring when you were overheard offering him a share, wasn't it?"

"It was." Minty produced the second bottle.

"And this partner of his?"

"A figtree of my imagination, sir."

"I thought as much." I fitted the bottles neatly into my tweed smuggling jacket. "One last thing, Mister Minter, if you will — I need limes."

"I can do you some grog."

"It has to be limes," I said. "I'm following a recipe."

"All out of limes, Mister Boisjoly." Minty sadly shook his head. "The captain took the last of them."

❦

"Oo-arr," drifted the captain's voice in reply to my knock. "Come in."

"What ho, Captain." I let myself into possibly the most cabiny cabin on *The Ballast*. It was what a captain's stateroom ought to be — outfitted in deep stained oak and bronze fittings, a waxed wooden floor that looked older than the ship, captain's chairs around a round table cluttered with charts and brass mechanical widgets of nautical utility.

There was even a coal-burning stove in black machinery iron on one side of which, perched on a lamp, was Albert Ross, and on the other, snug in a deep, richly worn chair and wearing bed flannels and a deep-pile dressing gown, was the captain.

"Evening, Mister...." He exhaled a plume of pipe smoke and focused hard on my face, as though reading it for signs of poor weather ahead. "Boisjoly?"

"The very same."

"You're very welcome, Mister Boisjoly. I regret, I have nothing to offer guests…" The captain looked around the room and then his eye settled sadly on a barrel in the corner. "Someone has had all me grog."

Albert Ross whistled his objection. "My grog."

"No, my grog," persisted the captain, "and it were me that drank it."

"It *was* me," amended the parrot.

"I don't need no bird defending me," scolded the captain. He aimed one frank eye at mine and, on finding it, avowed, "t'was me."

"Water, water, everywhere, and all the boards did shrink; Water, water, everywhere, nor any drop to drink," I appropriated. "Happily, Captain, I came prepared for just such an eventuality." I withdrew a bottle of brandy from my pocket.

The captain pushed out of his chair and staggered to a mantle above the table from which hung several pewter tankards.

"Just a small one, I think." Slapton endeavoured to wink at me, I expect, but settled on a lengthy blink, instead. "I've already had a few." He opened the bottle and filled his mug to the brim, such that the next tip of the ship, no less than 30 degrees north by 45 degrees west, spilled exactly a third.

"How long do you expect this to last, Captain?" I asked.

"You mean, split between the two of us?"

"I was referring to the storm."

"Oh. Arr." Slapton nodded knowingly and swallowed his brandy whole. "Till morning, and she'll get worse afore she gets better."

The storm roared agreement to the sentiment and then emphasised it with a new addition to the repertoire — thick, thumping thunder and lashes of lightning.

"But we're safe here on Squall Atoll," I hoped.

"Oh, arr... no." The captain shook his head at his tankard, which he then refilled and took back to his leather lair. "But here is where we'll longest remain right way up."

I made myself a modest mixer and pulled a captain's chair next to the crackling coal fire.

"Did I ever tells you how this atoll come to have its name?" slurred Slapton.

140

"Yes."

"T'was ought six," he continued, nevertheless. "I was pilot aboard *The Lucky*, a two-mast trawler out of old Grimsby. Seven souls aboard, bloodless with avarice and longing to ship their fill of sole from the rich pickings to be had in the Irish Sea."

"Irish Sea?" I queried.

"Aye..." Slapton swallowed a fortifying mouthful of brandy. "I'm coming to that."

I topped up his tankard and spared the bottle my own share.

"The wind was calm as death and the fog as thick as swill," continued Slapton. "We picked our way around the sound till I was solid certain we were in open sea — but then a many-coloured omen landed on our yard-arm; 'veer to port' quoth he."

"Are we talking about the parrot?"

"Macaw," Albert Ross insisted.

"Aye..." Slapton's eyes glazed over. Or, quite possibly, they had already been amply glazed. "Out of the mist he flew, landed on the main yard, and advised me to come to port. Every sailor's sense said no — follow the compass, follow the charts, follow the sun or common sense. But the bird, he spoke with otherworldly sight denied mortal eyes; 'veer to port' quoth he."

"And so you veered to port," I presumed.

"One doesn't just ignore otherworldly sight, Mister Boisjoly." Slapton shot a sharp glance that missed me by a good six inches. "A sailor would know that."

"Sorry. Carry on."

"Then the bird — he just flew away, into the mist," marvelled Slapton. "In time, according to his will, he come back, from out of the very beyond. Whenever I'd steady me course, he'd fly out of the drizzle and haze and settle on the yard. Then he'd catch my eye and speak straight to me; 'veer to port' quoth he. Again and again."

"Didn't that just turn you in a circle?"

"More of a wide arc," refined the captain. "The bird was unspecific as regards degree or course. T'was more a general advisory to come to port, and so in time we ended in the outer Scillies."

"Did the crew not object?"

"When they noticed that we were not in the Irish Sea, yes, they did most strenuously object." The captain nodded with melancholy recollection at his tankard.

"When they noticed?"

"Arr." The captain applied brandy to the wound. "Soon after they cast the trawling net, and it stuck on a reef."

"That sounds tremendously perilous."

"Can be," agreed Slapton. "If a squall, magnified by an atoll, comes at you broadside."

"Are we coming up now on how this atoll got its name?"

"Arr," arr'd the old captain with regret. "Very nearly capsized us." He tipped back his tankard, looked into the emptiness, and sighed. "The ironic thing is, what saved us was veering to port."

"Ah, well, then — you saved the ship."

"N'arr." Slapton held out his tankard for refreshing. "The men locked me in the galley with the bird. 'Let this Albert Ross always be 'round your neck,' they said."

"I think they meant albatross," I said as I refilled his tankard.

The captain endeavoured to focus on me a critical eye.

"It's a parrot."

"Macaw!"

"Aye," accepted Slapton. "Then there we were, in the galley, listening to the struggle between man and sea, and I asked him, I said 'Tell me, Albert Ross, why you wanted us to go to port. From what great tragedy did you save us, and for which you'll never get your due?' Do you know what he told me?"

"Veer to port?" I said.

"Aye." Slapton settled a weary eye on the bird. "Thems were all the words he knew, at the time."

"Those!" reminded Albert.

"Aye — at those time," said Slapton, chastised. "Then, for near ten years, I piloted the school boat between Tresco and Saint Mary's. Did Albert Ross's English no end of good, though he did learn some mighty bawdy shanties."

"Oh, right, talking of shandies, Captain, I need some limes."

"I was going to say..." commented Slapton. "A little sunshine wouldn't go amiss, neither."

"That's just the famous Boisjoly complexion," I explained. "The presiding family theory is that earlier generations were selectively bred to hide in snowbanks. Do you have any limes?"

"N'arr. Lady Hannibal-Pool took the last of them."

❧

Charlotte Lady Hannibal-Pool answered the door wearing one of those armoured housecoats with a collar that looks like a feather boa and panels of pearl-coloured silk that look bullet-proof. She was holding a silver porringer in one hand and a spoon in the other.

"Good evening, Anty." Lady H-P is one of those drinkers who, the more sloshed they get, the harder they work to present as sober. Very entertaining, as a rule. "Thank you so much for coming."

"You didn't actually invite me, Lady H-P," I reminded her. "I've just popped by to borrow a cup of limes."

"But of course." She shimmered away, taking the door with her. "Do come in."

The master stateroom was immense. Easily the size of two staterooms, judging by the reception room, which had four portal

143

windows and a full-sized dining table. It was strumped up along the geometric lines of the Art Deco theme of *The Ballast,* with bevelled chrome walls and riveted, aluminium furniture and lots of mysterious lighting behind cast smoked glass.

"His Lordship not in?"

Lottie blinked at me for a moment, smiling and swaying just out of time with the movement of the boat. Then she looked around the room.

"No." She dipped the spoon in the porringer and took a taste of something green and lumpy. "He's on deck... doing something yachty, I believe."

"Oh, right oh."

"You wished to sample the lime sour, I believe." Lottie had sashayed over to a silver punch bowl on the immense lacquered drinks cabinet. She withdrew a ladle from the bowl and took up another porringer. As she made a dive with the dipper, though, the boat heaved heavenward and the punch bowl, guardrailed by a smooth silver riser, slid to the other end of the cabinet. Lady Lottie followed it and as she caught up, naturally, the bowl slid back to my end. She trotted gamely after, but I held up a desist hand.

"Actually, Lady Hannipools, if you could just spare a single lime — I have very strict dietary requirements and something of a deadline."

Lottie furrowed her confusion into a single brow movement and stood holding her ladle while the punch bowl made another pass.

"But... there are no more limes. I've made them all into lime sour." She watched the bowl slide back to my end. "It's come out more of a pudding, in the end. I added almost all the grog we had and it's still the consistency of mushy peas." As the bowl slipped by again she dipped in a finger and withdrew it with a daub of what did indeed resemble mushy peas. She put the green blob in her mouth. "Quite tasty, though. It was a little tart..." here, for some reason she whispered, "...so I added a bit of grog."

144

Of all the desperate gourmands I know — and I have an uncle who, finding himself confined to a health spa, rolled a cigar of sun-dried tomatoes — Lady Hannibal-Pool is the very one I would think most capable of making an incendiary pudding onboard an all but unprovisioned yacht.

"Oh!" Lottie gave voice to sudden inspiration or bee-sting. "We must talk about your wedding banquet."

"My whating what-what?"

Lottie coyly ate a spoonful of green.

"You should know that I know, Anty — Winnie's read your letters to me."

"My letters? Oh, yes, of course. My letters. To your daughter. Winnie."

"You wrote it ever so many times — 'when we're married.'"

"When we're married?" I affected to cast my mind back. "Oh, yes, I see what you mean, it's really just an expression, though, isn't it, like 'well, I'm hanged', or 'when hell freezes over.'"

"Oh, hullo Anty." Lord Archie stumbled adventitiously through the door at this moment, bringing along that distinctive atmosphere of appreciated rum, last expressed so thoroughly and well by Minty. He was in a dripping slicker and thoroughly saturated cloth cap and inappropriate footwear which may once have been velveteen indoor espadrilles. "You here?"

"I am," I acknowledged. "I'm hunting limes, but I understand they've sacrificed themselves for the greener good."

"Not the peels." His Lordship delivered this message of hope as he divested himself of dampened rags and ex-espadrilles.

"That might do. In fact, it'll have to do. I'll take whatever you can spare."

"Just chucked them overboard," said Archie with the pride of one who knows not what he's done. "And we don't have much else to offer guests, I'm afraid…" He darted a glance at the punch bowl.

"Perhaps French distillers will come to the rescue, as they so often have before." I produced the bottle of brandy. "Snifty?"

Lord Archie bent forward and squinted at the label.

"Is that…" The floor teetered up and Archie backed away, then the floor tottered down and he quick-shuffled back. "…brandy?"

"It is."

"Where did it come from?"

"The Cognac region of France," I replied.

"I mean to say, where did it come from recently?" Archie and Lottie conspired to assemble the necessary glassware from the liquor cabinet and we convened in the lounge.

"You don't know?" I poured out three lifters of snifters. "I can assure you that the inspector is currently and uniquely uninterested in your live-and-let-live policy with regards His Majesty's customs officials."

Archie put a theatrical finger to his lips and issued a loud "ssshhhh."

"There's no contraband on *The Ballast* this trip, Anty — there's a policeman."

"I know."

"That's right." Archie pointed a prosecutorial finger in my rough direction. "You invited him. But here's something else, Anty — the Royal Mail charter is a legal fiction. This is the first trip we've ever made to Scilly."

"I know that, too," I said. "And so does Inspector Wittersham."

"Eh?"

"He worked it out. That's why he's on board. We've had this conversation once already."

"Oh, yes, that's right," realised Archie. "If he knew why didn't he just arrest me in Portsmouth and save all this dashed dashing about the Atlantic?"

"Because you're a peer of the realm, Lord H," I reminded him, "and you'd have almost certainly been on a nickname-basis with any presiding magistrate."

Archie looked to Lottie and then to me and then he drank from his snifter in a sort of amazed daze.

"How darkly cynical."

"You don't mean to say it's not true."

"Well, of course it's true, Anty, but you'll admit it's dreadfully cynical to act on the point," said Archie with the confident ire of the drunkenly defamed. "That's your modern policeman, for you."

"Is it worth all the trouble?"

"It's usually no trouble at all," offhanded Archie. "I don't typically have policemen on board. This was just going to be a little tour around the Isle of Wight, with an evening at Ventnor."

"In time for a full moon," added Lottie. "Very romantic."

"Yes, I understand that Caspar Starbuck ordered it up especially," I said.

"He did, that's true." Lottie rocked for a moment with the storm and meditated on this aspect of the lunar cycle. "I can't imagine he'd object, though, if you were to take the opportunity to recite a little poetry to Winnifred."

"I say…" I started that sentence without knowing where it was going, only that it must lead somewhere far away — Kensington, for example, "...what do you suppose my house is worth, Lord Archie?"

"The one in Kensington?"

"The very one," I confirmed. "It strikes me that it would fetch something similar to what you paid for your place, what?"

"Are you thinking of selling up?" asked Archie. "I always wondered what you were doing with a place that size."

"He needs it, Archie," snookered Lottie. "For when he and Winnie have children."

"So, nice little racket, is it, this Royal Mail caper?" I veered hard to port.

"It pays mooring at Portsmouth, Bristol, and Dover," accounted Archie. "Plus there's a bit of a retainer, although that's gone to pay two crews for this odyssey."

"You engaged Captain Slapton and Minty Moy especially for this journey, did you?"

"Commodore Bittleswill advised it," retrieved Archie through the fog of time and brandy. "Said a local pilot was the only way to navigate the Scilly seas with any measure of safety."

"And that would doubtless be how Dare Flashburn discovered that *The Ballast* was coming here."

"Stands to reason."

"But no one else would have known," I surmised. "Not Caspar nor Bunny?"

"Oh?" Lottie swayed affected indifference. "Is there a rabbit on board?"

"He means Harry Babbit," Archie disappointed her racing culinary ambitions. "Can't see how they could know we were going to Prosperity Skerry."

CHAPTER SIXTEEN

A Wary Wherry to a Scarey Skerry

At five in the morning the thunder and lightning sputtered out. By six o'clock the wind had whooped itself down from a wild whistle to a wistful woosh. Soon after, the sea settled and *The Ballast* levelled and, somewhere, a seabird revelled the morn. At six-thirty the engines grunted and roared and then grumbled long and deep like they hadn't eaten in days.

"What's that?" asked Ivor.

"The engines, I believe," I replied through the haze of a sleepless night. "I expect the captain and Minty are casting off for Prosperity Skerry. I'll just run up and stop them. Will you be all right with no one to moan at for five minutes?"

It had been a trying night. The vault and walt of the waves had visited upon Ivor spectres and ordeals and memories of pies he'd eaten as a young constable just starting out and, in his British policeman's sense of fair play, he had shared his pain generously with all Boisjolys within whinge-shot. I'd endeavoured to pass Lottie's lime sour and a quart of whisky off as a concentrated version of the old family seasick medicine but Ivor insisted it only made him feel worse, which is undoubtedly true, given that it was just lime sour and a quart of whisky. Now, in addition to being seasick, the man had a crippling hangover.

"Run up...?" stounded Ivor. "And stop them?"

"From going to Prosperity Skerry," I said, enlarging as much as was possible on the theme of stopping. "You said last night that we mustn't land until we've found the second map."

"Land..." Ivor spoke the word with much the same tone of hope and awe with which I've heard Lady Hannibal-Pool say 'mutton chop'. "Solid, unmoving, reliable, constant, land."

"Yes, land, Inspector, technically, but it's just Prosperity Skerry. A barren and dangerous rock."

"Rock..." Ivor, who was in one of the many contortions that he'd tested during the night, withdrew his head from beneath the nightstand. "What a firm, friendly word. 'Rock.' Tell me more about this rock, Boisjoly."

The engines hit a high note and Ivor fitted his head back under the night stand as the boat juttered in reverse and we pulled out of our sanctuary on Squall Atoll. I sought the crisp morning air, and along the corridor mustered a weary, bleary gallery of reflections of the Boisjoly burden.

"What, uhm, ho, Anty." Teddy appeared at the door of her cabin, wearing a blue satin dressing gown the wrong way out and holding a snifter of ice water. "I do wish you'd come back last night. I finished off that brandy alone, and then went to your cabin looking for you and found only a bottle of Glen Glennegie."

"Perfectly all right," I assured her. "I have another in my boot box."

"Not anymore you don't. Is it morning?"

"After a fashion. They start them much earlier at sea."

The next door along the hall opened and Winnifred, a notorious thimbler with the draught of a pedalo, hung out a harried head of hurried hair, and blinked at us.

"Anty?" she spotted as her eyes finally began operating as a team. She then touched her hair once and then again to satisfy herself of the full horror of the situation, said "Ack," and ducked back inside her cabin. Only a drifting puff of down and dust remained.

"Poor petal," commented Teddy. "I could hear her through the walls last night, singing *It Had To Be You.* Both parts." She frowned at the ceiling. "Or was that me?"

I left Teddy to brush off the night and lighten it with lipstick, and as I passed his door Caspar appeared, looking at least as raw and remorseful as everyone else.

"Morning, Anty." He rather underdelivered this, with the breathy whistle of a brass section composed of a tin flute. He cleared his throat, and then said it again the exact same way.

"Morning, Capsize," I greeted. "You look as though you finally slipped off the wagon and rolled down the hill into the canal."

"I suppose I did, rather, yes," whispered Caspar. "Any idea where we're going?"

"Prosperity Skerry, I expect," I said. "Those were the last stated instructions of Inspector Wittersham before the seasick cure wore off."

"It wears off?" queried Caspar. "I thought it was a placebo."

"It was, but it was a placebo treatment, not a placebo vaccine." I looked warily back at Ivor's door and lowered my voice. "As we're always saying in the imaginary pharmaceuticals game — there's no bad medication, only bad presentation. I'll refine the formula for future doses."

"I'll see you up top." Caspar faded back into his cabin and I continued to the end of the corridor and the Hannibal-Pool doss-box, which accordingly opened as I passed.

"Who's that?" said Lottie in a wary hush.

"Just your dear old Anty Boisjoly, Lady HP."

"What time is it?" Lottie spoke as one not willing to fully embrace the miracle of morning.

"Coming up on seven, I think."

"But it's so dark."

"Still wearing the sleeping mask, LPH," I reminded her.

"Anty," she realised as she removed the night blinders. "Did you drink much of that lime sour?"

"Sadly, there wasn't quite enough to go around."

"Just as well." Lottie massaged a head of upright hair. "I think there may have been something off about it — I don't feel at all well this morning."

"Something going about the ship, I expect. I've seen a lot of it." I nodded sagely. "The brandy was all right though, was it?"

"Oh, yes, the brandy was excellent."

"Morning, Anty." His Lordship appeared behind Lottie, poorly wrapped for morning in a threadbare dressing gown. "Where are we going?"

"Prosperity Skerry, I expect."

"What?" Archie fumbled with his robe like a man who, under the influence of strong drink, has forgotten how robes work. "That lunatic on the island will sink us."

"I was just on my way to discuss that very point with the captain."

"I'll see you up there."

Bunny was the next patient. We met at the exit to the main deck, from whence he was just tottering, wearing the tailored three-piece I'd seen him in the previous evening, but it was pulled and undone and hitched in the tradition of the direct-from-the-cells court appearance.

"Oh, what ho, Anty." We negotiated passage through the door. "Just going for a bit of a lie-down, if you'd be so kind as to pick a side."

"Have you been up all night?"

"I don't know." Bunny looked about us for, I suppose, a clock. "What time is it?"

"Seven or so."

"Then yes, I've been up all night." Bunny leaned against the door frame in a manner suggestive of one who doesn't know he's leaning against something. "Just had to defeat that dashed billiards table."

"And did you?"

"There were a few moments when I thought I had it sussed," he claimed. "I know it's something to do with timing the crescendo of the wave with the speed of the descent and angle of the cue ball relative to the red and, I expect, the horizon, but if anything the poxing game only got more difficult as the night wore on. Doubtless it was down to the unpredictability of the storm."

"Nothing to do with the keg of grog with which you clearly arrived at easy terms."

"Course not, Anty. Got the constitution of a lead-lined goat, you know that. Anyway, now the storm's stopped the challenge has gone out of it, and I thought I'd get some kip."

"Right oh. I'll have Vickers give you a shout if we sink."

"Is that likely?"

"We're approaching Prosperity Skerry and its single attraction — a man and his cannon."

"I'll be right up."

The ship's bell clanged and the engines ran at a low hum as the fog parted before us like a curtain. Prosperity Skerry lay dead ahead, cold and black and lifeless, its edges stitched with white foam. A long, steely glimmer cracked the horizon in the east and skipped on furrows and folds across the expanse of the sea. The timbers of *The Ballast* creaked and cricked and met the waves with a rhythmic whish and wash.

"Full stop, Mister Moy," Captain Slapton ordered into the speaking tube.

I had joined him in the great, glassy rampart of the bridge reasoning that, if we were to be fired upon from shore, I might just as well see it coming.

Slapton was appraising the threat through his telescope.

"No sign of the enemy gunner." He passed the device to me, and I put it to my judgemental eye.

The fog was rapidly lifting and a shard of morning illuminated the little coast. The schooner stood skeletal against the growing light, its spars swaying and its cannon, apparently, unmanned.

The door opened and Caspar stepped curtly in. He'd brought his own telescope, with which he now also surveyed the situation. "We appear to be just out of range, Captain."

"Oo-arr," agreed Slapton. "If the inspector still wants to row ashore he'll have to do it from here."

"The inspector's in no condition to lead a reconnaissance detail," pronounced Caspar. "I shall go ashore in the jolly boat with Mister Babbit."

The Babbit in question, at this moment, stepped through the door.

"Oddest thing," he said. "The jolly boat's gone."

"N'arr," contradicted Slapton. "She's main deck, starboard side."

"No, she isn't," contradicted Bunny just as well as he got. "Not if starboard is right, and in any case I've checked both sides. It's not there."

The captain stepped out the starboard side door of the bridge and a moment later returned.

"The storm must have blown her clean away." Slapton leaned once more to the speaking tube. "Engines forward full throttle, Mister Moy, we're heading for home."

"Belay that order!"

Ivor had appeared at, and supported by, the door. He presented an array of symptoms that were difficult for me to encapsulate, lacking any real expertise in wet rot. But the comparatively calm seas and

154

simultaneous drive to stand on dry land had given him a decidedly wobbly but serviceable authority.

"Belay that order, I say, in the name of King Arthur."

"King George," squawked Albert Ross.

"King George," amended Ivor. "We're seeing this investigation through."

"On your head be it then, Inspector." Slapton turned to the speaking tube. "Dead slow ahead, Mister Moy."

"You can keep an eye on the cannon, Mister Starbuck," said Ivor. "And if there's any sign of danger we'll withdraw. Mister Boisjoly, I'll ask you to fly the flag of truce from the bow."

I had a quick rummage in the dining room and settled on a smart silver tablecloth, and brought it with me to the bow. The distance had closed considerably by the time I was waving the tablecloth at, for all I could see, an uninhabited island.

There was a nostalgic element to my contribution, transporting me to a time when Cook would put me in charge of watching the flour to stop it escaping or, when positions were distributed for football, I'd be made a linesman. Nevertheless, my role put me in a position to observe that which the others might not through the narrow ambit of the telescope.

As we approached the tiny harbour I could see that it was embellished with a small wooden dock, to which was moored the little two-masted schooner. There was no one on board and the cannon posed no threat.

The cove was a natural haven, protected from the elements by smooth walls of weather-worn rock on three sides, and some sort of edifice — a fishing hut or smoke house or, quite possibly, some rocks and weatherboard that had been swept together by the elements — had been put to some recent purpose.

We had been approaching in a cautious sort of arc, as far astern as was practical of the loud, smoky end of the cannon. As we rounded the natural shelter, the depth of the cove came fully into view, revealing that which caused me to drop my tablecloth into the sea — moored to a piling was the landing boat of *RMS Ballast.*

The engines stopped. In time, Minty appeared on deck, treading a narrow path, as one whose head weighed some unknowable amount more than expected. He lowered himself down onto the tiny, tippy dock and moored us to a piling such that *The Ballast* was bow-to-stern with the little two-rigger, and he tied off a rope-and-slat gangway.

Ivor was a changed man. The moment he stepped onto the comparative stability of the dock he ceased to be a doddering, desperate invalid and became, in an instant, a Scotland Yard Inspector with decision and authority and an iron-bar hangover.

He and Minty determined that the jolly boat — christened *RMS Ballast Jolly Boat* — was indeed ours.

"Most curious," pronounced Ivor.

"Perhaps the storm washed it here," I proposed.

"And tied it to the dock?"

"Must have been the bloke what lives on the island done it," pointed out Minty. "Seems oblivious, when you think on it."

"He's right, Inspector," I said. "It is oblivious, when you think on it."

"Why don't we find him and ask him." Ivor drummed up the dock to the rocky shore. I followed.

"Hello?" Ivor sidled up to the door of the shack. Silence. The only reply was the soft whistle of the breeze and rhythmic rush of the seas and Anty's knocking knees.

"I say, Inspector," I reminded him in my 'let's sneak out during the third act for a cheeky short one at the intermission bar' voice, "he might well be armed, and he's got form with firearms."

Ivor peered through the open door, then raised himself in that 'stand down' manner indicative that a danger has passed.

I joined him at the door. The danger had indeed passed, as had the poor chap on the floor, by all appearances with the aid of a blunt instrument.

CHAPTER SEVENTEEN

The View of the Isle from Pilyek Pile

"Blunt instrument," confirmed Ivor.

We looked around the little room. It was modest, even by the standards of the storm shelters of the outer Scillies, but there was nevertheless a surprisingly large number of instruments that could be described as blunt. One chair (broken), blocks of coal (scattered), a shovel, a pickaxe, selected hammers (from one for peening to several for sledging), one telescope (brass), and a broad selection of rocks (round). There was also a small travel trunk that had been pried open and one could presume that the papers and clothes and bits of personal ephemera scattered about the floor had once been within.

"You think the killer found it?" asked Ivor.

"Happiness?"

"The second map."

"You think he was looking for the second map, Inspector?"

"Don't you?"

"Quite possibly," I acknowledged. "What I wonder, though, is why anyone would think it would be here."

"Because this chap was looking for the treasure, very obviously." Ivor set about sifting and sorting the papers.

"But if he has the map, why hasn't he found the treasure?" I asked. "And if he found the treasure, why is he still here? It's a delightful destination, certainly, but limited in terms of entertainment possibilities for a man with a fortune in gold."

"Well, there are no maps here, in any case." Ivor put the papers into a serviceably flippable form. "Mainly correspondence...blimey, there's a coincidence."

"Was he writing to Winnifred Hannibal-Pool too?"

"His name..." Ivor passed me an envelope. It and the letter inside were addressed to a chap in Bristol called Talbot Starbuck.

"Rather a lot of that going around." I gave the letter a quick butcher's. "It's a reply, accepting a share of the treasure in exchange for supporting Talbot's claim to it."

"Hullo." Teddy appeared at the door. She had cleverly camouflaged her condition in navy whites, complete with blue and white ribbon-striped trousers, but that only served to make her hangover look as though it was at an early rehearsal of *All Hands*. She cocked her head at the form on the floor. "Who's that then?"

I said, "We're not sure," for some reason, and slid the letter into my inside jacket pocket.

"Why are you not on the boat, Miss Quillfeather?" asked Ivor.

"Was I meant to be on the boat?" she asked, well within reason. "We're docked. I'm seeing the sights. Might get my hair done. Take in a show."

"Yes, well, if you wouldn't mind, hold the line at this shack," instructed Ivor. "No one's to go beyond the cove nor come in here, is that understood?"

"Right oh, Inspector," agreed Teddy. "I can go in though, can I?"

"No."

"I just want a bit of a lie-down. I think I might have eaten something funny last night." Teddy tapped her tummy tellingly. "Can't think what else it might be."

"No. Mister Boisjoly, if you'll accompany me..."

Ivor plucked up the telescope and stalked out of the shack. He led to the edge of the flats that comprised downtown Prosperity Skerry.

"We're going up there." Ivor pointed with his eyes — like Lillian Gish registering 'wistful' — at Pilyek Pile.

"Would it not be wiser to wait a bit, Inspector?" I regarded the craggy, jaggy incline. "Say, until they build a funicular?"

"We're agreed, I take it, that even if someone were able to make it through that storm last night in a landing boat, he clearly didn't make it back."

"Yes, agreed, but everyone is accounted for. I was able to do a full census this morning before we docked."

"Were you?"

"It's engraved indelibly on my memory." I reflected on the gauntlet of hard mornings I passed on the way to the bridge.

"Then have you considered, Mister Boisjoly, that there's one improbability that explains all the others?"

"A stowaway."

"Yes," said Ivor, with a sprig of pique. "A stowaway."

"Yes. I considered the possibility."

"He must be on this island." Ivor continued up the mound. "And we can see the entirety of it from atop this hill."

This much, it turned out, was true. The top of Pilyek Pile was a pointy, perilous plateau of scrabbling pebbles, affording an expansive view of the oblong skerry and its jagged coast for a mile in any direction, after which the world was a settled mist of gently shifting gossamer.

"Spotted him?" It's nigh on impossible to say certain things unironically. Like when you ask a chap if his barber's still in prison or if he can remember whose round it is — he's bound to think there's a subtext. This was an excellent case in point — as Ivor traced the coastline with his telescope, I could see with the naked eye that it was a barren, hedgeless, Skegness of a place with no crease nor crimp in which to hide a small-to-medium-sized stowaway. The Roman Graveyard was identifiable as a few raised rectangles of stone around a natural circular depression in which water had accumulated to form that which was doubtless the rainwater well. The Viking village could be seen, with a squint and a tremendous imagination and enthusiasm for Vikings, in a couple of stone foundations on the flats of the cove. The rest of the island was extruded effluence of volcano, splashed out aeons ago and now standing static as the unremittant sea wears it away again.

"He's on that schooner," concluded Ivor.

"I don't think he is, Inspector," I differed. "Observe the electric whir on the deck. That's Lady Hannibal-Pool, searching the vessel for stores of exotic spices or ice cream. If there had been anyone hiding on board he'd have been found by now."

Ivor monitored Lady Lottie for a moment, then lowered his telescope.

"Another boat altogether?" wondered Ivor.

"Seems improbable," I said. "Any boat big enough to weather the storm would have been too big to moor anywhere near the island. No, Inspector, what we have is the most vexing case of locked-island murder I've ever encountered."

"Yes, very well, Mister Boisjoly, we definitely have two impossible murders and no credible suspect." Ivor raised his telescope again and observed the passengers and crew of *The Ballast*. "I guess we're back to this lot." He collapsed the telescope and put it in his pocket and economised on the action by withdrawing his pipe. "Very obviously your cousin, Theodora, is at the top of the list."

I scanned the party of passengers gathered about the dock. Teddy was not among them and had presumably ignored Ivor's instruction to not go into the shack for a lie-down.

"She'd be honoured, Inspector," I accepted on her behalf, "but Teddy has no instinct for unkind acts at all. She did once, long ago when happiness was measured in sunny summer days, convince me to jump off the potting shed, but I like to think that she honestly believed that the lace parasol would slow my descent."

"She had the map."

"Dare gave it to her."

"According to her." Ivor puffed up his pipe to dramatic effect as the smoke swirled about us in the wind.

"It was right there on her wall, Inspector," I cited.

"Did you notice it, or did she draw your attention to it?"

"Doubtless she'd have raised the point in time," I said. "We had some important brandy issues to settle first."

"And how do you know she doesn't have the second map? She might well have put the first map on display as a distraction."

"That is, in fact, exactly what she'd have done, if she were the sort of young lady who goes about biffing treasure hunters with blunt objects," I said coolly, "and so that's exactly what she did not do. Besides, she was fully distilled last night when Talbot Starbuck saw his last storm at sea."

"Assuming that's true, she might have had an accomplice." Ivor nodded meaningfully at Winnifred who, having evidently capitulated to the overwhelming forces of morning head and hair, was wearing a turban. She stood on the deck, smoking without benefit of a cigarette holder and drinking tea and looking as though she abhorred both activities.

"Not really an accomplice sort of strategist, our Teddy," I said. "More of a gardener — planting little seeds of fib and fable and, with patience and periodical spadework, allowing them to sprout into a cracking caper. She read the classics at Oxford and her final thesis was a rhyming-couplet ballad retelling of Machiavelli's *The Prince.*"

"Then, of course, there's His Lordship." Ivor aimed the stem of his pipe at Lord Archie, still in his threadbare housecoat, teetering on the dock and watching Lottie and rehydrating himself from a glass gourd.

"Also amply brandied," I testified. "Not to mention fully grogged and even lightly limed."

"Well he's got a built-in accomplice, hasn't he."

"Lady Charlotte?" I followed Ivor's line of sight to Lady Hannibal-Pool, the only cast member displaying anything like initiative, though even she was holding one eye closed and regularly pausing her search to lean against a mast, and she was wearing her husband's slicker over a nightgown. "She might blacken your eye in a fair fight over the last profiterole, but I can assure you that she wouldn't kill for anything short of a New Year's reservation at The Ritz. In any case, Lady Lottie, too, was slurring her garbling even before I visited them last night."

"Could have been an act."

"If it was, it was a showstopper," I said. "I'll also observe that the Hannibal-Pools lack anything like a motive."

"The treasure, obviously."

"The Hannibal-Pools don't need any more treasure, Inspector," I scoffed. "They're pennyroyaled, to the rims. Last year Lord Archie had to be reminded that he owned an entire town in Surrey."

"I believe I've already expressed my views on the notion of innocence by wealth." Ivor grimaced through his cloud at Lord Archie's private yacht. "In any case, His Lordship had another, more base reason to kill."

"For a laugh?"

"Revenge, Mister Boisjoly," puffed Ivor. "Did you not wonder why I asked you to get me invited on this journey?"

"It wasn't to catch up with an old friend, free of the distraction of murder?" I asked. "Now see how that worked out."

"Scotland Yard received information from an anonymous source that Lord Hannibal-Pool was thimblerigging The Royal Mail," said Ivor. "And when you later mentioned that you knew him, and had been on the very yacht in question, I seized the opportunity to put an end to it."

"Yes, I already know that you abused our friendship."

"That's not the question."

"It's *a* question."

"Clearly, it was Dare Flashburn who informed Scotland Yard about the unfulfilled mail charter, with a view to obliging Lord Hannibal-Pool to take him to Prosperity Skerry," continued Ivor. "Equally clearly, it was Mister Flashburn who sent the letter, timed to be at the post office in Grimsby when we arrived."

"Yes, that does sound convincing," I conceded. "Except for one, tiny detail."

"Which is?"

"It's unadulterated twaddle," I replied. "The Royal Mail charter is an economy to Lord Archie, nothing more. Admittedly, his little economies mean a great deal to His Lordship, but in the main as collectables. He kept his flat in Mayfair for a year after he was married so he wouldn't have to pay to have his mail diverted. And even setting that aside, the Hannibal-Pools are still well short of a motive to murder Talbot Starbuck."

"I think it probable that Mister Starbuck also knew about the fraud." Ivor smoked defiantly at the gathering in the cove. "He clearly knew that he wasn't receiving any mail."

"Fair enough, but let us examine some possibilities grounded in reality. You may find it relevant, for instance, that the hold of *The Ballast* is full of trunks, barrels, and sacks of contraband."

"I may find it relevant?" Ivor's eyebrow rose remonstratively.

"Furthermore, Dare Flashburn knew about it," I continued. "And he used this knowledge to extort several bottles of brandy out of Minty."

"I see."

"Mind you, so did I."

We both sought sight of Minty in the bustling port of Prosperity Skerry and found him, finally, at the end of the dock, staring into the sea and reinforcing the spirit with a tin cup of, I suspect, hair of the dog.

"He tells me that the captain was in on it," I said. "I told him that you'd be happy to overlook it."

"You did, did you?"

"In a non-committal sort of way," I assured him. "I expect you could still get a couple of bottles out of it."

"Either way, it's hardly a motive for murder," said Ivor. "And certainly nothing to do with Talbot Starbuck."

"Talking of Talbot Starbuck, what are we making of his surname?"

"Yes, I've been reflecting on that." Ivor gazed down at Caspar, Captain Slapton and Albert Ross, standing on the shore, evaluating the horizon and settling some maritime matter of grave import. "Could be coincidence."

"Starbuck?" I said. "It's hardly a common name, Inspector, like Smith or Boisjoly."

"You think he knew about the treasure?"

"He said that the legend of the sinking of John Mucknell's ship was family lore," I recalled. "And, indeed, that there was a First Mate Starbuck on one of the ships that participated in the engagement, but he failed to mention that it was *The Phoenix,* the ship that stole away with the treasure."

"So, certainly a candidate."

"He also made a very distinct point of claiming that there was no treasure," I added. "And furthermore that Dare shared that view."

"When was this?"

"Yesterday, after we all got back from Grimsby," I recounted. "The smart set met in Dare's cabin for brandy and banter."

"I see…"

"I know what you're thinking, Inspector," I said. "I thought that too — but Teddy insists that they tried to invite me."

"How long were they there?" Ivor squinted at a notion floating in the smog of his pipe.

"An hour or so. They were knackered from running back from Cromwell's Castle."

"Which means that Dare Flashburn was seen alive after the Hannibal-Pools boarded at Hugh Town," mused Ivor. "And at least an hour after we locked the trunk in my cabin."

"By all accounts, yes."

"So, everyone on board, but the trunk locked — in chains — in my cabin." Ivor knocked out his pipe on a rock. "A murder everyone would have committed, but nobody could have committed."

There's something concretely final about the knocking out of a pipe, so I took a last look around the island, which really amounted to little more than a craggy, cracked brim of rocky tendrils around Pilyek Pile, hosting a graveyard for what must have been some not particularly well-liked Romans and a community of very lonely Vikings.

"It occurs to me, Inspector, that not only is there nowhere to hide a stowaway," I observed, "there's no obvious place to hide any amount of treasure, either."

"Surely if it were obvious it wouldn't be much of a hiding place," noted Ivor.

"But it's meant to be thousands of gold ducats. There's an inventory among the documents that Dare got in Shanghai."

"And?"

"It's just got me thinking of something else…" I withdrew the letter that we'd found earlier, addressed to Talbot Starbuck. "Why would this chap have a claim on the treasure?"

"Why would anyone?"

"Exactly." I unfolded the document and, this time, turned it over. "Caspar told me that there were rumours that John Mucknell's descendants had changed the family name to some variation of the name."

"Such as?"

I passed Ivor the letter, and surveyed the scene at the cove, where Bunny was sitting on a coil of rope with his head in his hands.

Ivor read the salutation, "It's signed Peter Dunghill."

CHAPTER EIGHTEEN

Cardall's Clever Cure-All

"Henry Babbit's real name is Dunghill?" marvelled Ivor as we skidded back down the hill.

"No, his real name is Babbit, but it used to be Dunghill until, for perhaps obvious reasons, he changed it."

"Just as some forebear changed it from Mucknell to Dunghill," deduced Ivor. "Can't be a coincidence that there are two descendants of the crews of *The John* and *The Phoenix* on this voyage."

"No, it does seem meaningful, somehow, doesn't it?" I agreed. "Note, however, that Bunny said that he spent the entirety of last night preparing for the boat billiards national championships and reducing the world's net supply of grog."

"Do you believe it?"

"Judging by the state of him, yes," I said. "In fact he presented this morning as a chap coming off a second shift of court-ordered debauchery."

"Was anyone not drunk last night?"

"Not a one," I said. "And that includes you. You called me Anty."

"I have no recollection," whisked Ivor. "I was delirious with seasick."

"And a quart of whisky," I fondly recalled. "You also said, incidentally, that we mustn't disembark at Prosperity Skerry, or there'd be another murder."

"I said that?"

"It would be very helpful if you could remember why."

"Well, I can't," said Ivor. "Does that seasick remedy really call for so much whisky?"

"I might as well tell you now, Inspector, that there's no such thing as a seasick remedy."

"Of course there is," insisted Ivor. "It just wore off."

"No, what wore off was the wholly psychological effect. It was a placebo."

"A placebo."

"Or sawbone's bitter, if you like," I added, for I know the inspector dotes on detail. "It's as the liquid courage of the Cowardly Lion — you had the sea legs beneath you all along."

"You didn't see fit to mention this last night, during the storm, while I suffered agonies?"

"Would it have helped?"

"It would have helped a good deal more than a quart of whisky."

"Oh, I don't know, Inspector. It afforded us an opportunity to air some important personal issues," I reminisced. "I know I feel much lighter."

"There's no seasick medicine." Ivor had stopped on the incline and was staring out to sea in the manner of a Caravaggio epiphany or Vickers trying to recall why he's in the coal cellar.

"Actually, Inspector, there is," I disclosed. "Let me tell you about this chap at my club, Spins Purley…"

"Please no, Mister Boisjoly."

"You'll like this one, Inspector," I plugged. "You see, Spins had the mal-de-mer far worse than you."

"I find that difficult to believe."

"No, I confess, that does seem a bit fanciful, doesn't it?" I agreed. "Let us say that while his symptoms may not have been as severe as your own, they were debilitating and, obviously, hilarious. He once conceded a trophy match at his golf club because playing to the sixteenth hole would have required crossing a bridge over the water hazard."

"Yes, very well, Mister Boisjoly. Spins had an extreme case."

"On carvery days he has to look away when we pass the gravy boat."

"But you say that he found a solution," pressed Ivor.

"By exigent circumstance," I reported. "Mrs Purley — delightful woman; face of an angel, legs of a chorus girl, annuity of a Vanderbilt — and all she ever asked of Spins was two weeks every summer, to romance and to frolic in the remote and bucolic countryside of Provence."

"In France."

"The one in France, yes," I confirmed. "You can see poor Spins' dilemma."

"The channel crossing."

"He couldn't say no to his better half by half, neither could he see the sea," I said. "The answer came from the most unlikely source — Euchre Cardall."

"Yes, that does sound improbable."

"He's a real chap at my club," I maintained. "He is herein described as 'unlikely' because he and Spins are bitter rivals. It was Spins who seized the prestigious chair of the Juniper tablecloth committee — a role that Euchre had held for eight years — in a hotly contested election, and it was Euchre who spread the rumour that Spins had done so by exploiting links to London's criminal underworld. It was Euchre who, charged with the arrangements for the gala spat and garter awards — an event at which Spins is an annual favourite for at least a silver buckle — organised it as a boat trip on the Thames. It was Spins who introduced a rule to the umbrella games outlawing the practice of an opponent opening his device during the fencing round — Euchre's signature move."

Ivor was relighting his pipe.

"And it was Euchre who had first been engaged to Mrs Purley," I concluded.

"I understand, Mister Boisjoly, they were bitter rivals," idled Ivor. "So what changed?"

"Nothing changed at all, Inspector," I said. "They were still clubmates and hence outside of their rivalry they were as loyal as any two brothers. When Euchre heard of Spins' predicament he offered the couple his own little chalet and, equally importantly, he suggested the treatment for Spins' mal-de-mer."

"Which is?" Ivor's interest and eyebrows rose to heights unprecedented for this anecdote.

"A sleeping draught," I replied. "Entirely natural, completely effective. The patient awakes refreshed and alert and insensible to the passage of time."

"I doubt even that would have worked for me." Ivor, in his disappointment, looked out at the menacing waves.

"You misunderstand me, Inspector," I said. "The sleeping draught wasn't for Spins, it was for Mrs Purley, and the cottage was in the Cotswolds."

"Of course."

"Euchre rechristened it *'La gite legite'*."

"Did Mrs Purley not notice that all the neighbours were English?" doubted Ivor.

"The only establishment for miles around is a pub — The King's Head or, once Euchre had purchased it, *La noggin du roy,*" I said. "The patrons are all English, which is about right for a pub in Provence, and Euchre staffed it with Belgians who, you doubtless know, will work for chips and beer anywhere it's not constantly raining."

We had arrived at the edge of the flats of Skerry Cove when Ivor seized my arm.

"Boisjoly..." he spoke in a soft stifle. "I recall what I said last night."

"Calling me Anty, you mean?"

"No, I have no recollection of that." Ivor settled a studying eye on the passengers and crew milling about the cove. "I remember why I said that we mustn't disembark here."

"Oh, right oh," I said. "Why?"

"It's as you said when we were on top of the hill — if there's still someone on the island then the treasure must still be on the island, too," plagiarised Ivor. "And if someone's willing to kill for it, once he's got it, he's not going to want to share it, and he'll be even more dangerous if he's discovered."

"Yes, good point, well made," I agreed. "In that instance, Inspector, I may have some bad news for you."

"What is it?"

"I've worked out who killed Dare Flashburn and Talbot Starbuck, and how it was done."

CHAPTER NINETEEN

The Measure of Whether the Treasure is Nether

"Captain Slapton killed Dare Flashburn and Talbot Starbuck," I revealed. "And he did it for the treasure, because he's been an underpaid and skint part-time school-boat pilot ever since nearly capsizing a fishing boat in 'ought-six because he let a parrot navigate."

"You're drunk."

"It's mainly worn off," I wibbled, "but I haven't slept in two days. Nevertheless, I know that Captain Slapton did the murders because he's the only one who could have."

"How did he do it?"

"There are two Grimsbys on the island of Tresco," I said. "Between you and me, I feel that one was more than ample, but unless I'm very much mistaken one of them is called New Grimsby and the other…"

"Old Grimsby." At that point, doubtless, Ivor recalled the local directing us to 'old' Grimsby post office.

"While we docked in New Grimsby, you were too seasick to notice and I was too preoccupied with your tortures to suspect that we weren't just anchored off Hugh Town," I continued. "That was when Dare, Teddy, Bunny, and Caspar visited Cromwell Castle. They had to run back, significantly, to be on board by eight bells."

"But that's when we got back," objected Ivor. "Eight bells."

"Recall that Slapton and Albert Ross differed over the watch — there's more than one. We returned by eight bells of the afternoon watch," I guessed. "Dare and Teddy and Bunny and Caspar's eight bells were the previous watch — four hours earlier, when Minty was filling the hold with contraband."

We looked to the dock. Minty was still there, but now he was sitting on a piling, openly drinking from a bottle of brandy and, occasionally, scrutinising it with one eye to judge how much was left.

"He told me that Slapton was participating in the smuggling, but the captain had no idea how I'd acquired a bottle of brandy," I recounted. "I should have made the connection then."

"We were distracted by my state, fair enough," noted Ivor. "But how could the others not notice the time difference?"

"What time difference?" I asked. "When everyone was in New Grimsby you and I were sleeping off a turbulent night. We assumed that our seven bells and their seven bells were the same seven bells, and the only people on board who knew otherwise had solid reason to prevent us from realising that there were two Grimsbys — Slapton, because it made his crime appear impossible, and Minty, because he went ashore in New Grimsby, which is an historically lively smuggler's port, to collect a shipment of cognac."

"I thought that Caspian Starbuck came from some proud naval tradition."

"Exactly," I said. "Which is why he wouldn't admit to the reason why he and Bunny lied about their activities — Caspar has seasickness. Look at him now…"

Caspar was standing in the town square of the Viking village, inflating his lungs and singing *Rule, Britannia.*

"…on board he's a stiff who won't take a drink, sits in the dark with the curtains drawn, and expresses a theatrically casual interest in the Boisjoly family seasick remedy. He was sick as a braxy mutton, and Bunny was spontaneously covering for his friend, which is why their stories didn't quite match."

"So, Slapton went to Dare's stateroom while we were at the post office in Grimsby," reasoned Ivor.

"Old Grimsby."

"Old Grimsby. He killed him and took the second map…"

"And then he hid the body in a trunk in the ship's store, doubtless intending to drop it overboard during the night," I added. "But when we showed up with a similar trunk he led us to the store room. In the brief time before you decided it would be better off under your direct supervision, it was lost in the darkness."

"It was only a moment."

"That's all he needed," I said. "You'll recall that Minty distracted us — he simply wanted to prevent us seeing how crowded the hold had become. Meanwhile Slapton was alone in the store with the fishermen — he took the opportunity to chalk 'Ballast' on the trunk containing the body, and then he simply told the boys to take it to your cabin."

"But… the letter," objected Ivor. "It was in the trunk."

"Slapton put it there when he and Minty shifted the body to a lower cabin."

Ivor stoked up a dense cloud of pipe smoke suitable for nodding and squinting.

"Yes, it's the only way it could have happened." Ivor's atmosphere swirled and thickened. "But, how did he get to the island in the middle of the storm, kill Talbot, and return to the ship?"

I gave him a moment to come to the light.

Presently, Ivor's haze of smoke was whisked away on the wind.

"The cottage in the Cotswolds."

"Exactly," I confirmed. "We were never docked on Squall Atoll, at all."

"It was Slapton who said there was no safe mooring anywhere else on Prosperity Skerry," continued Ivor. "He just sailed us into the fog and around the other side of the island."

"And at his leisure, walked here and murdered Talbot Starbuck."

"And took the treasure."

"No."

"No?"

"No," I repeated. "Again, I don't think Talbot had the treasure, or he would have left with it."

"But Slapton has the second map," connected Ivor. "He must have used it to find the treasure last night."

"He might have the second map, but I don't think he was able to find the treasure."

"Why do you say that?"

"The jolly boat." I nodded towards the dock. "The treasure is immense and immensely heavy. Slapton hauled the jolly boat here by tow rope, with the intention of using it to get the gold, or at least some of it, back to *The Ballast*. The fact that the jolly boat is still here tells me that the treasure is, too."

"What a startlingly poor plan," judged Ivor.

"It is, but it may not be as intricately inept as it appears," I suggested. "I think that Slapton initially planned to steal the map and only resorted to the slap-dash hysteric's weapon of choice, the blunt object, when he discovered that Dare was on board. After that point of no return, he assumed that we'd sail for home, allowing him to come looking for the treasure at some later, safer date. But when we carried on regardless and he learned that Talbot Starbuck was already here, he felt he had no choice but to act."

"So he's bashing together his strategy moment to moment."

"I think it fair to presume that Captain Slapton's next moves will be entertainingly erratic, yes."

We searched the cove for the captain.

"He must be on board," presumed Ivor.

The sea, it's worth noting, was beginning once again to assert itself, and *The Ballast* was twisting on its moorings.

"What ho, Ants, Spex." Teddy popped out of the shelter with a steaming cup of something in her hand. "Did you find the treasure?"

"We were looking for the stowaway," I reported in.

"There's never any stowaway." Teddy blew a sceptical head of steam off her cup. "That would have meant this whole thing was planned and, speaking as one with a modest history of successful campaigns, I can tell you that this bowl of scrambled second thoughts was the opposite of planned."

"Quite right," I acknowledged. "We arrived at the same conclusion."

"Did you also work out that it was Captain Slapton who did for the guy in the shack?"

"How could you possibly know that?" asked Ivor.

"Well, I don't, for a concrete fact, but I know that Caspar didn't do it because he is, beneath that dreary hull of barnacles and British reserve, a big old plush penguin, and he and the captain are the only ones among us who aren't, each in our own way, nursing hardwood hangovers."

"Confirmed," I said. "Last night when I went to his cabin he claimed to have been drinking all night, but had to take tankards down from the wall for the brandy and, unlike Minty and the Hannibal-Pools, he exuded no fog of grog."

"I assume we were really docked on the other side of the island," said Teddy.

"Correct again. Is that coffee?"

"No."

"I was very clear, Miss Quillfeather," bristled Ivor. "No one was to go into the shack."

"What ho, Anty, Inspector." Bunny stepped out of the shack with a steaming cup of his own.

"We were looking for the treasure," punted Teddy. "I was thinking, how could we be most helpful."

"There's a body in there," pointed out Ivor.

"We covered him with a blanket," said Caspar from the door, a steaming coffee in his hand.

"Do you by any chance recognise him, Mister Starbuck?"

"Ehm, yes. I do."

"You do?" Ivor paused the relighting of the enquiry pipe. "I take it then that it's not a coincidence you're both here."

"Talbot Starbuck is a distant cousin," Caspar finally disclosed with a minute but meaningful emphasis on the adjective. "A bit of an eccentric. He's been obsessed with the treasure of *The John* for years."

"You knew that it was he who fired a cannon at us," concluded Ivor.

"There won't have been a cannonball," deflected Caspar. "He was trying to warn us off. I had rather hoped that it would work myself."

"Would you care to explain your presence here, Mister Starbuck?" asked Ivor without really asking.

"Not if it could be at all avoided, no."

"It can't."

"No, I suppose not." Caspar took a steadying draw on his coffee. "Talbot has been pursuing clues and conspiracies regarding the disposition of the treasure for years, ventures he financed by periodically extorting a contribution from the family."

"By what menace?" I asked.

"Well, the very story, obviously, Anty," said Caspar. "We've been Royal Navy for centuries, with nary a lost ship nor mutiny. The family would be scandalised if it became known that we'd had a first mate aboard *The Phoenix* — not even a royal privateer, but pirates who betrayed their own."

"That doesn't explain your presence," contended Ivor.

"It does, in fact," said Caspar. "Every year or so, one of us has to come out to Prosperity Skerry and bring Talbot in. He's been here for two months, this time. This year it was my turn to lead a delegation, but for my own reasons I couldn't set out to sea with any members of my family."

"You have seasickness," revealed Ivor.

"Ah. You know."

"We do," Ivor assured him.

"Yes, well, my family doesn't," said Caspar. "I convinced them that it would be more discreet for me to voyage as a guest of Lord and Lady Hannibal-Pool, about whose Royal Mail charter I knew through naval contacts."

"You sent the letter addressed to Prosperity Skerry," I surmised.

"I did, yes," confessed Caspar. "And I also sent a note to Scotland Yard, informing them that *RMS Ballast* had never delivered any mail to the outer Scillies."

Ivor puffed pensively, and then pointed his pipe at Bunny.

"And Mister Babbit, obviously, is your co-conspirator."

"Eh? Me? Why?"

"For the same reason as Mister Starbuck," said Ivor. "To protect the secret of your descendancy from Captain John Mucknell."

"I'm not descended from John Mucknell."

"Actually, Bunny, you are," said Caspar. "The surviving line changed the name to Dunghill in 1652."

"Well, fancy that."

"You didn't know?" doubted Ivor.

"If I had, so would have everyone else."

"Then, your presence here really is just a coincidence?"

"Not entirely," clarified Caspar. "I contrived to befriend you at Oxford, initially, to find out how much you knew or might learn about the participation of the Starbucks in the betrayal of John Mucknell"

"Not really."

"I'm afraid so, Bunny, old man."

"You abused our friendship for the sake of your family's reputation?"

"Yes."

"Oh, well, fair enough." Bunny sipped the casual coffee of the loyal friend. "Happy to help."

"Would you care for more coffee, Miss?" Vickers now appeared at the door of the shelter with a tin camp pot.

"Cheers, Vicks." Teddy held out her cup and Vickers obliged.

"There's no more sugar, Vickers." Winnifred whinged into view. "And the powdered milk is making lumps in the coffee."

"How big is that shack?" I asked.

"There is an ample rear extension, sir." Vickers handed me a tin cup and filled it. "First Mate Moy is stoking the fire."

"Are you calling for me, Mister Vickers?" Minty emerged now with a tin cup of brandied coffee.

"First Mate Moy," spoke the authority of Scotland Yard. "Where is Captain Slapton?"

"On *The Ballast,* sir," replied Minty. "In the store room."

"How do you know that he's in the store room, specifically?" I asked.

"I deducted it, sir, on account of him taking the key off me."

"And Lord and Lady Hannibal-Pool?"

"I believe they're on board, too," reported Minty.

"Right, well, they should be safe enough — you should all know that we believe that Captain Slapton murdered Dare Flashburn and Talbot Starbuck."

There was a general nodding agreement, verbalised by Caspar, "Yes, Teddy told us."

"There's no cause for concern," continued Ivor. "He has no weapon and while he's shown himself capable of desperate acts, he must also know that he's now without option apart from peaceful surrender to my custody."

In that instant Slapton materialised on the main deck, from which he hopped down onto the dock. He wandered towards us with the casual gait of the unsuspected and slightly tipsy.

"Arrr, Inspector." The captain, unaccompanied by Albert Ross, expressed himself freely. "I expect you've worked out by now t'was me what done for them two poor men."

"We have," said Ivor. "If you'll give me your word that there'll be no trouble, we can dispense with manacles for the return voyage."

"There's just one thing needs doing first, Inspector."

"Which is?"

"You see, sir, I done what I done for the treasure, but in the end I was unable to find it."

"All for nothing, then," moralised Ivor.

"So far, that's so," agreed Slapton. "But it don't have to be that way. So I propose we strikes us a bargain…"

"Absolutely not, Captain," quashed Ivor. "The treasure, if it's still here somewhere, belongs to the crown."

"The king don't need all of it, though," argued Slapton. "And I'll only take what I can carry in that there sloop." Slapton gestured towards Talbot's two-rigger.

"Why would we agree to such a thing?" Caspar wanted to know.

"I'm very glad you asked, sir." Slapton addressed all of us. "If you'll find that second map and then the treasure, and put as much of it on that boat as she'll hold, well then, I give you my word of honour as a man of the sea that when I'm a mile out I'll signal flag the combination to the lockbox on the bridge."

"What possible use could that be to us?" protested Bunny.

"It's where I put the keys, sir," Slapton patiently explained. "And you'll be wanting them soon enough, because I locked the Hannibal-Pools in the ship's store."

"To what end?" asked Ivor.

"I believe I've already outlined the essentials, Inspector," piqued Slapton. "And, so we're all of us on the beam with respect to the pressing nature of matters, I have scuttled *The Ballast*. She's sinking."

CHAPTER TWENTY

The Seamless Scheme of the Scheme Unseen within the Seeming Scheme

To the untrained eye of the clubbing Boisjoly, *RMS Ballast* looked in top nick. I did note, now that Captain Slapton had made such a sudden and sober study of the boat, that it had sneaked away a bit on the current, as though she was inching toward the pub door before anyone noticed that it was her round.

Caspar, however, gave it a single glance and agreed, "She's sinking. She's already beginning to list to starboard, and he must have loosed her moorings — she's floating away."

"I'll have that combination, if you please, Captain." Bunny began removing his jacket.

"You should know that I've taken the precaution of downing half a bottle of brandy," warned Slapton. "Your time would be better spent searching for the treasure."

"Mister Babbit, take the jolly boat and board that ship," ordered Ivor. "Mister Moy, go with him. Have that door down whatever you have to do."

Bunny and Minty dashed down to the dock.

"Mister Boisjoly, in the meantime…"

"I'll do what I can, Inspector, but do I understand you to say, Captain, that you don't have the second map?" I redirected.

"N'arr." Slapton shook his head with baffled regret. "I never found it in Flashburn's cabin nor here."

"Miss Quillfeather, if you have the second map, now is the time to say so," said Ivor.

"I only have the one he gave me," insisted Teddy.

"That's not the first map," I said. "Dare made that one."

"What makes you say that?" asked Ivor.

"Squall Atoll. It's on the map hanging on Teddy's wall, but in 1645 it was an unnamed outcropping," I reported. "In fact, it wasn't called Squall Atoll until Captain Slapton's trawler hooked its net on it in 1906."

"Arr, that be true."

"The map isn't a map at all — it's a ballad in linked sonnets, recounting the night Mucknell's ship fought three parliamentary warships, and then transferred the gold in its hold to *The Phoenix.*"

"But it only says where *The Phoenix* went," said Teddy. "Not where the treasure is hidden."

"Exactly," I concurred. "Do you recall what the journal said about the chap who made the maps — he worked in the theatre. There was never a second map — there's a second poem."

Ivor withdrew the papers we'd found in the shack.

"There's nothing like that here."

"There wouldn't be," I said. "If Talbot had the second poem he'd have worked out the location of the treasure by now."

"So, it's lost," lamented Teddy.

"Anty, please..." pleaded Winnie with a novel sort of whatsit in her voice — humanity. "You're ever so clever, and you know all about poetry. You can work it out." Then she addressed Caspar, but directed her attention to Slapton. "Meantime, this big bloke can hold the captain's head under water until he gives up the combination to the lockbox."

"Anty..." trailed Teddy. "Why do you say it's a sonnet?"

"Because it is," I said. "In the Shakespearean style. Three quatrains and a couplet."

"How does it go again?" wondered Teddy.

"Ehm.

A ship so something something calloused
She sailed for somewhere, something ballast…"

"Right, but it's a sonnet, you said," Teddy reminded us. "Three quatrains — three verses of four lines of alternating rhyming scheme, followed by a couplet. It went something like

A ship so beaten up and calloused
And just loaded down with whales
She sailed for home, for home at last
With very white and pretty sails"

"You can't possibly be serious." Winnie swallowed the last of her coffee and sort of assumed centre stage. She drew in her breath like a diva and recited…

"A ship so battle-worn and calloused
With a draught up to her gunwales
She sailed for home with gold for ballast
And ribbons where were once sails

When three barks of the commonwealth
On course for the isles of the outer seas
Barred her from her home and help
She tacked a course towards all three

A thousand times she ran out her guns
As the Phoenix watched the fires dim
Then signalled 'stay, we've just begun'
And she trimmed her mizzen in

Then she quit the fire and smoke still settling
By wind, by fortune, and by dead reckoning

But as sea rushed in at either side
She picked her passage through the shoals
She hobbled home and there she died
And finally loosed her cursed load

Within sight of Saint Mary's lee
Where the gathered pool is calm
She finally slip't beneath the sea
Where ancient sailors meet their gods

Her final act to disgorge her gold
The riches that low cunning made
Into the pirate traitor's hold
From then on that's where they stayed

Where did The Phoenix finally go?
To her nest on the isle of Prospero"

"Blimey." It was Ivor who said that but it was a generally held sentiment.

"Did you hear it, Anty?" asked Teddy. "It's a rubbish sonnet, because it's not a sonnet at all — it's two poems — in rhyming couplets — superimposed. When it's a linked sonnet, it seems to just tell the tale of the sinking of *The John*. As rhyming couplets, it tells a completely different story."

"Both maps hidden in plain sight," I summarised.

"Exactly," enthused Teddy. "Winnie — can you do it again, but this time do every first and third line, and then again with every second and fourth."

"Of course," said Winnie, as one stating the obvious.
"A ship so battle-worn and calloused
She sailed for home with gold for ballast
When three barks of the commonwealth
Barred her from her home and help

186

A thousand times she ran out her guns
Then signalled 'stay, we've just begun'
But as sea rushed in at either side
She hobbled home and there she died

Within sight of Saint Mary's lee
She finally slip't beneath the sea
Her final act to disgorge her gold
Into the pirate traitor's hold

As The Phoenix watched the fires dim
And she trimmed her mizzen in
Then she quit the fire and smoke still settling
By wind, by fortune, and by dead reckoning"

"Well," I said. "That makes much more sense — this bit is about *The Phoenix* leaving the scene."

Freddy continued...

"Where did The Phoenix finally go?
To her nest on the isle of Prospero
With a draught up to her gunwales
And ribbons where were once sails

"'With a draught up to her gunwales' because she was full to bursting with gold," deduced Teddy. "And tattered sails because, as we learned from the account of the signalman of *The John*, Captain Mucknell shot at her rigging to prevent her from going far."

"On course for the isles of the outer seas
She tacked a course towards all three
She picked her passage through the shoals
And finally loosed her cursed load

"It's not *The John* tacking towards three parliamentary ships," I interpreted. "It's *The Phoenix* making for the three outer Scilly islands."

Where the gathered pool is calm
Where ancient sailors meet their gods
The riches that low cunning made
From then on that's where they stayed"

"And 'where ancient sailors meet their gods' isn't the bottom of the sea," twigged Teddy. "It's the Roman graveyard here on the island. What's this about a gathered pool?"

"The rainwater well, in the middle of the graveyard," I said. "We saw it from the top of the hill."

"The treasure is down the well!"

"Oh, do come along, Anty," protested Caspar. "You can't believe that you worked out in five minutes what Talbot couldn't over the course of years."

"He didn't have the map," I suggested as an explanation for this admittedly sensational development.

"Or an actual, literal deadline," added Teddy. "Shall we debate the point, Caspar, or go look in the well?"

So it was that Caspar, Teddy, and I scrambled up Pilyek Pile. Caspar took a very unsportsmanlike lead and was down the other side when Teddy and I reached the top. I took the opportunity to assess the situation at sea. *The Ballast* was turning freely in the livening eddies and whirls and there was no one on deck, but the jolly boat was tied off and, presumably, Bunny and Minty were endeavouring to break down the store room door.

On the other side, Caspar was at the edge of the rainwater well in the Roman graveyard, staring into it at something which brought an awe to his typically teakwood features.

"There's nothing here." Caspar was glaring his disappointment at the well's shortcomings as we approached.

His meaning was clear as the water in the well. It was a shallow basin, a natural depression in the rocky surface, and there was very obviously no treasure.

"Just a tick…" Teddy, who was on the other side of the well from Caspar and me, squatted and squinted. "There's a sort of shelf of rock. Who knows how far back it goes."

Caspar positioned himself to dive into the shallows but Teddy stopped him.

"You're too big and blocky, Caspar, we'd never get you back out again." Teddy took his place. "Hold my feet." And in she went.

"What a remarkable woman," observed Caspar, as we stood on the bank, fishing with my cousin.

"You should see her cheat at croquet," I advised him. "I expect it's exactly the way DaVinci used to cheat at croquet."

Some subtlety in her movement indicated that Teddy was reaching for something deep within the shelf. Presently, she raised a hand, and we pulled her out of the water.

"I have never been so cold in my entire life," announced Teddy. "And I found this."

In her hand, somehow shimmering in the grey gloom, was a silver coin.

"The bad news is that it's one of three," said Teddy. "The rest is gone."

"Extraordinary." Caspar took the coin from her hand. "So Talbot was right all along… just too late."

"May I see that, Caspars?" I received the coin and examined both sides. "Possibly," I said. "But this is an Edward VII shilling, issued in 1908."

"Eh?"

"Worth approximately a shilling, would be my guess," I said.

A clamour and whoop, of the urgent and instructional tone one associates with football terraces, came to us from all directions. We scrabbled back up the hill.

There had been developments.

Bunny was on the deck of *The Ballast,* standing heroic and, somehow, taller. Lord Archie was on the bridge, as nettled as I've ever seen any peer of the realm. On the dock, Ivor had received a mooring line from Bunny and was regarding it with suspicion.

More eventful still, the two-rigger had half a sail unfurled, and was putting to sea.

By the time we reached him, Ivor had become a serviceable dockworker, and was just tying off the rope gangway.

"Minty's stopped up the hole in the hull with a sail." Bunny stood on the deck, his hands on his hips and his chin pointing towards further worlds to conquer. "I knocked the store room door down with an axe."

"Is this vessel sea-worthy?" Ivor wanted to know, judging by his tone, instantly.

"It is," assessed Caspar. "The hole can't have been very big, and a sail-cloth patch will hold well enough."

"Everyone on board," commanded Ivor. Slapton's sloop was now at full sail and was turning into a strong easterly wind.

"Was it there?" asked Ivor as he followed me up the gangway.

"It never was," I replied.

"Engines ahead full, Mister Moy." Caspar assumed command of the yacht and his seasickness in a single stroke of willpower. He stood tall on the bridge, barking orders into the speaking tube and spinning the wheel to turn a tight twist out of the sharp narrows of Prosperity Skerry. Soon we were in the open sea and pursuing Slapton's sheets into the eastern mist.

"Can we overtake him, Mister Starbuck?" asked Ivor, who also by all appearances had chosen mind over malady.

"Of course," boomed Caspar.

"No," booed Lord Archie. "We're returning to Saint Mary's. *The Ballast* is in no state to participate in a naval action."

"Of course she is," cheered Caspar. "She handles like a porpoise."

And in that instant the engines went quiet, and *The Ballast* slowed to a stop.

"Mister Moy…" Caspar addressed a self-possessed impatience to the speaking tube. "Full ahead, if you please."

There was no reply from Minty for some considerable time, and then he appeared at the door.

"The engine room is flooded, sir."

"Flooded?" staggered Lord Archie. "Flooded with what?"

"Seawater, Your Lordship," said Minty. "Up to me knees, sir, but it's ample to choke the engines."

"Can you pump them out?" asked Caspar.

"Aye, sir. Soon as I repair the hull."

"Can you repair the hull?" asked Archie.

"Aye sir," said Minty. "Soon as we get her into dry dock."

"So, we're stranded," desponded Archie.

"Aye sir," agreed Minty. "And we're sinking again, faster than ever."

CHAPTER TWENTY-ONE

The Twist Missed
in the Mist

"Bunny, Lord Archie," barked Caspar, "get to the hold and jettison the lot. Everything not actually part of the boat goes overboard."

"I should just like to point out, sir," pointed out Minty. "That everything in the hold marked 'grog' is indefensible."

"Indispensable," squawked Albert Ross.

"Nothing's indispensable," countermanded Caspar. "We have to raise the hull above the leak or at the very least reduce our draught."

"And then what?" complained Archie.

"Then we get under sail," said Caspar. "Mister Moy, shake out the mainsail to beam reach and trim the mizzen as hard as you like to counter the list."

"Aye aye, sir."

"Is all this necessary, Mister Starbuck?" asked Ivor. "I can still see Prosperity Skerry."

"We're not going to Prosperity Skerry, Inspector." Caspar tied off the wheel and turned to the charts. "We're going to Saint Mary's."

"You don't think that's too far to go with a hole in the hull?"

"It's the closest viable port, Inspector," replied Caspar. "Without a local pilot and drawing the draught we are now, we couldn't possibly clear the reefs around Prosperity Skerry. Our only chance is to make for Saint Mary's Harbour."

Minty set forth to make sail, and Bunny and Lord Archie to ruin Minty financially. I kept carefully out of the way with my eye to the telescope, internally rehearsing my 'land, ho!' Before and below us on the prow, Ivor was braced by the air and unmoved by the waves, like a figurehead of Neptune smoking a pipe.

Port side of the main deck, her curls wet and wild and her shimmer dress deliberately torn at the knee to increase manoeuvrability, Winnifred was receiving cases of brandy from Bunny and heaving them into the sea. Lady Hannibal-Pool was discharging the same function on the starboard side. Teddy was with us on the bridge, teaching Albert Ross a bawdy limerick. Caspar stood at the wheel, facing down the fates and commanding by will and wheel *The Ballast* to push through the waves, listing so far to lee that one could see only sea slipping by the starboard windows.

We skidded against the crosswind, Caspar tacking and jibing according to some twitch of breeze picked up by his beard. This dragged on and on and Caspar never tired, but in time, it seemed, *RMS Ballast* did. With no land in sight, the boat was now moving with all the grace and glide of a cow wading through a bog.

In time the sails began to give and then snap and crack like gunshots, and on each such occasion the boat shuddered and slowed and the sea at the starboard window got closer and closer.

"We won't make it." Caspar spoke with what would have been a handsome defiance, had he been talking strictly of his own watery grave.

"I say, Caspar, I can't be sure, but I think I see land."

"You do." He nodded at the grey silhouette in the fog. "I mean to say that we're not going to make it as far as Saint Mary's Harbour." He slapped the wheel to port and bounced us once again off the wind. "We're going to Porth Cressa."

"Port Cressa?"

"Porth Cressa." Caspar gestured at the charts. "It's a bay on the south end of the island."

The bow of *The Ballast* was now, even to my amateur eye, heavy in the water, and kicking up great plumes of foam against waves with an agenda wholly opposed to ours.

"I endorse this Porth Cressa plan," I said. "Sounds a delightful place."

"It's too shallow for *The Ballast,*" said Caspar. "I'm going to run her aground."

In that instant we burst through the screen of mist. The island quickly consumed our entire horizon and the visual and visceral effect was that we were now moving at tremendous speed.

The sails shivered and *The Ballast* shuddered its length. The timbers squealed against one another and I could feel the structure loosening beneath our feet.

Caspar nudged us slightly toward a dark patch of water ahead, something which we both hoped was a soft and sympathetic sandbar.

"Tell all hands to brace themselves." Caspar leaned forwards as though willing the boat to go faster, and I think it did. I leaned out the door of the bridge to repeat Caspar's warning as the dark patch of water raced towards us.

"Veer to port! Veer to port!" squawked Albert Ross, and Caspar, for some reason, did just that. He cranked the wheel counterclockwise until it would move no more. The mast and the hull screeched in protest. *The Ballast* leaned almost vertical as she twisted on a tether. For a flash of a moment I was looking directly into the sea on the starboard side at the razor reef that had been posing as an innocent sandbar.

With a great flumpy sort of floof, almost exactly like the sound of a bag of flour emptying over the head of an Oxford vice-chancellor, we thumped to a dead stop. The deck was angled acutely and the starboard side was fully submerged, but anything that could have rolled off had done so hours ago, and the passengers were securely stowed. We had safely run aground.

❦

The Fisherman's Rest was a homey, stony tavern of low, beamed ceilings, lumpy heaps of warm, worn rugs, a blazing coal brazier the size of a wine barrel, a multitude of misshapen windows framing a pastoral picture of Saint Mary's Harbour, and the best wine list for twenty-five leagues in any direction. Great communal pots of stargazy pie and fried cod and chips were laid out on elbow-smoothed oak tables as thick as a mast. All hands were gathered in the warmth, wrapped in loans of blankets and cable-knit sweaters and scarves. The atmosphere was a gathering of dizzy relief, a festive feeling fuelled by the intoxicating ether of narrow survival.

I contemplated the harbour through the spatters of rain on the window pane, aided in the exercise by a glass of merlot — the grape variety bred especially for meditations on the existential metaphors presented by rainy harbours.

Also musing on the philosophical implications of drizzle and piers was Lord Archie, leaning against a window frame and swirling a neat whisky and wondering what it's all about.

"Chin up, Your Lordship," I prescribed. "It's all insured, isn't it?"

"Hmmm," hmmm'd Archie in the affirmative, and then searched the ceiling for an evasive, invasive thought. "I think I own the insurance company."

"Then you're in a position to save yourself a bit of money," I said, for I know His Lordship's weaknesses.

"Eh? How's that?"

"You'll want to salvage *The Ballast* as cheaply as possible. Get someone on site straight away, someone who knows the vessel..."

"Who?"

"Oh, that I couldn't say... Oh, what ho, Minty."

Minty had wandered over in response to my subtly waving for him to wander over. Of the range of options offered by the Fisherman's Rest, he had a glass of grog in his hand and Albert Ross on his shoulder.

"Oh, here's Minty." I casually observed. "Minty, Lord Hannibal-Pool has a pressing need for a reliable first mate."

"I'll give it some thought, sir." Minty massaged his chin. "Reliable first mates is very scary."

"Scarce!" exasperated Albert Ross.

"Scarce, aye." Minty nodded to the authority on his shoulder.

"Well, what about you, Minty?" I suggested.

"I understood you to say 'reliable'."

"You performed your duties with aplomb, I thought."

"I thank you, sir." Minty acknowledged the tribute with a tip of his tankard. "But I've often been held back in my chosen field owing to instances of excommunication."

"Miscommunication," revised the bird.

"Miscommunication," Minty happily repeated.

"The solution to that problem, Minty, sits on your shoulder," I said. "Have you any other obstacles to honest employment?"

"Well, sir, there's the smuggling."

"Are you prepared to give that up?" I asked.

"No, sir."

"Excellent," I lauded. "Neither is Lord Hannibal-Pool. You'll make excellent co-conspirators. And *RMS Ballast,* when she's once again afloat, comes with the ideal cover — a charter from the Royal Mail for the outer Scillies."

"Can you start salvage operations today, Minty?" asked Lord Archie.

"The sooner we have her sea-worthy, Your Lordship, the sooner we can recover what we can of that which was chucked over the side."

Minty gave a smart salute which Albert Ross deftly dodged, and tacked for the door.

Lady HP joined us then. She was wrapped in a deep shawl and smiling happily at a basket of whitebait that she carried with her like a newborn.

"Anty, you poor, dear sweet boy…"

"What ho, Lady Lottie."

"It's time we discussed you and Winnifred. Hold this…" She handed me her basket of bitty battered bunts and cleaned her fingers on her shawl.

"No rush," I assured her. "It can wait till we're back in London. We should get together at the next coronation."

"Anty, you need to cease paying your addresses to our daughter." She took back the basket and offered it around.

"Oh…" I sought the trap hidden behind these honeyed words. "Right oh."

"You'll get over it, in time."

"Doubtless. If I could just have one more smelt…" I selected a consolation whitebait, "…there, all better."

Lord and Lady Hannibal-Pool went once more into the breach of the buffet and I glided on air to the bar, by which stood my impish cousin Quillfeather with a glass of wine and a smug dial of the sort that she sports when she's successfully brought chaos where once there was calm.

"I say, Tedds, breaking news from Boisjoly central…"

"Lord and Lady Hannibal-Pool have asked you to stick to your side of Kensington, and free Winnifred to explore other options?" guessed Teddy.

"Ehm. Yes," I said. "Well?"

"Hmmm?"

"How did you work it?" I wanted to know for purely academic reasons. This is how one learns.

"They think you've lost your money."

"Not really," I gogged. "How?"

"How do they think you lost your money or how do they come to think you lost your money?" specified Teddy. "Closely related, I admit, but not the same question."

"Dealer's choice."

"I told them that you'd invested everything in a scheme to build a whisky pipeline between Spey and London."

"They didn't believe that," I doubted.

"Worryingly quickly," differed Teddy. "Particularly when you asked Lord Archie what he thought you could get for your house in today's market."

"Of course." I toasted Teddy's tactic. "I appreciate it very much. Mind you, it was the least you could do."

"Oh, well, you're very welcome, I'm sure."

"Enough of that, Teddles. I recognised the Theodora Quillfeather fang-marks from the outset," I said. "You deliberately gave me Winnifred's address at the auto club and let me think it was Freddy's."

"Then why did you write to her?"

"I say outset," I revised. "I mean I picked up on it this afternoon, when I recalled that you also told me that she was going to be on board *The Ballast.*"

"It was for the greater good," tall-taled Teddy. "Bash Postcombe is absolutely hatters and hare for Freddy."

"I'm hatters and hare for Freddy."

"No, you're not." Teddy adjusted my scarf affectionately. "You're infatuated with her, just like you are Penelope Doncaster and Stel Digby."

"Not Stella anymore," I updated. "She's allergic to oysters."

"Bash asked me to help him move things along with Freddy, and Freddy expressed similar sentiments with regards to the shy but otherwise quite affable Bash," continued Teddy. "So I got us box seats at *Funny Face* and I got you an innocent diversion."

"Innocent?" I marvelled. "I nearly had to marry the Winds of Whinge."

"And now you don't." Teddy pointed with her glass at Bunny. He was in a borrowed cable-knit fisherman's sweater that hung on his shoulders like an avalanche. With him was Winnifred, who hung on his arm like an avid branch. "You're welcome."

"That falls neatly in line with your aspirations for this trip, I think."

"Pure coincidence," said Teddy. "Although, now you raise the point, Caspar is taking to the sea. He's currently at the dock, arranging a vessel on which he and Inspector Wittersham are going to pursue the captain."

And then, just as in rehearsals, the door of the taproom swung open and Caspar established a beachhead. He had found himself a pea jacket and high rubber boots and a demeanour of energetic urgency.

"Good news, Inspector..." Caspar swept a tankard from a hook on the wall and dipped it into the grog pot. "...Boatload of fishermen, trawling for sole, spotted Slapton's boat wrecked on a reef at Squall Atoll."

"Where is he now?" asked Ivor.

"Squall Atoll," answered Caspar. "The trawler — boat called *The Lucky* — had form with the captain and the chaps took some pleasure in leaving him where he was."

"Did you get us a boat?"

"Three mast sloop called *Scilly Sue.*" Caspar drank in a Minty manner from his tankard. "She'll be crewed and outfitted by six bells of the morning watch."

"Are you tempted to go looking for the treasure, too?" I asked.

"I rather think not. It's long gone." Caspar searched his pocket. "Apart from this." He held out the three shillings we'd found in the well. "Salvage rights are yours, Your Lordship, by law of the sea."

Archie happily snatched up the coins.

"Pre-1920 shillings," he enthused. "Ninety-two percent silver."

"Eh?" Caspar paused his drinking arm. "Silver?"

"Mostly, yes."

"Then, these may not have just been dropped by whoever recovered the treasure," he speculated. "Talbot put them there."

"Why would he do that?" asked Lord Archie.

"Rudimentary water purification. Silver is a natural antibacterial agent. The practice was often used in the age of sail to keep the drinking water pure. Or any rate as pure as could be hoped in those conditions."

"However the coins got into the well," I announced, "they weren't dropped by whoever took the treasure."

"Why do you say that?" asked Ivor.

"Because the treasure was never in the well," I sipped my merlot meaningfully. "It was never on Prosperity Skerry."

"How could you possibly know that?" wanted to know several people at once.

"It was marked on the map," pointed out Caspar.

"A map that was made centuries later by someone interpreting what he thought was one of two poems," I said. "He looked at the three islands on a chart — one nameless, at the time, one called Sneaky Reef, and one called Prosperity Skerry. The only and obvious candidate for the Isle of Prospero was Prosperity Skerry."

"*The Tempest,*" twigged Teddy.

"Exactly. Oh, thank you, Vickers." I paused here for Vickers to refill my glass, and for effect. *"The Tempest,* by Shakespeare, tells the tale of Prospero, who is marooned on an island by a storm.

Recall that the original, overlapping poems were hidden in a Shakespearean sonnet by a theatre clerk."

"Well then, what was the name of Prospero's Island?" was, once again, a common and broadly held point of interest.

"It was nameless."

A strategy session formed of the representatives of the respective sea-faring families. I withdrew to the calm of the brazier, by which stood Ivor with a warm brandy and cold stare. We had to speak in our windy day voices to be heard over the din.

"Bon voyage, Inspector," I hailed. "I'll have Vickers mix you up a keg of seafood remedy."

"That wouldn't be necessary even if it weren't a placebo," claimed Ivor. "I want to thank you for that, Mister Boisjoly — I feel completely free of my mal-de-mer."

"I think that may have had more to do with the more pressing threat of being dashed to death on the rocks," I speculated.

"Quite probably," agreed Ivor. "In any case, I feel quite prepared to take to sea with Mister Starbuck."

"Is Bunny joining you?"

"I believe so." Ivor cast an eye at Bunny, who was miming for Winnifred's benefit how he felled the door of the store room with an axe.

"I was impressed by how quick Mister Babbit was to forgive when he learned that Mister Starbuck had ulterior motives for making his acquaintance at Oxford," said Ivor.

"Initially, perhaps, but they've since become friends," I homilied. "Certain things transcend college and class and club."

"Yes… Listen, Boisjoly, I regret taking advantage of the mutual regard we have for one another."

"You mean our friendship?" I asked. "And I'm sorry I gave you a quart of whisky on rough seas instead of telling you that the seasick medicine was a placebo."

"Call it square, then, shall we?"

"Spoken like a gentleman." I raised a glass to the diplomatic breakthrough. "You still have no recollection of what you said last night?"

"No, sadly. Was it in any way pertinent to the case?"

"Not this one, no." I mused on my merlot. "Mostly indictments of the privileged class. You said we ought to hang the king."

"I said nothing of the sort."

"And abolish the monarchy altogether."

"Tosh."

"I thought you couldn't recall."

"I know that I would never have said that." Ivor regarded Lord Archie who, in that moment, was in talks with the hostess of the Fisherman's Rest, negotiating a volume discount on chips. "Maybe the House of Lords."

"So, we're not a throughly and thoroughly corrupt class."

"No, not all of you," allowed Ivor. "Some of you are salvageable."

"Right oh, Inspector." I left him, then, so that I might consult with Vickers regarding our near-term wardrobe requirements. As I walked away, I heard Inspector Wittersham whisper just beneath the buzz,

"You're a good chap, Anty."

Aft.

Thank you for reading *Mystery and Malice aboard RMS Ballast*. I hope you didn't work out too quickly how it was done and by whom, and that you regardless enjoyed the voyage. I'm never, ever sure if I'm pushing the boat out too far, but I confess that I was charmed by the idea of a body found locked inside a sea chest long before I worked out how that could possibly happen.

This story is entirely my fault and I'm not spreading the blame when I say that the details of the real Captain John Mucknell come in part from the findings and theories of diver Todd Stevens, described in his book *Pirate John Mucknell & the hunt for the wreck of the John*. Mucknell really was a privateer and he really did steal a ship which really did end her days in 1645 in a battle with parliamentary forces, somewhere near the Scilly Islands, and Mr Stevens proposes an exciting theory about how Mucknell managed to survive to command another ship.

So we finally have a pirate number. We also have a brief breakdown of the wall between Anty and Ivor and we have Teddy Quillfeather who, as a personality, has been with me for almost as long as Anty Boisjoly. They're obviously very similar — they're both of the idle upper classes in the best possible age in which to pursue the profession and they're clever and quick and witty and slick.

But Teddy is not a female Anty Boisjoly. Where Anty's capricious, she's mischievous, where Anty's deductive, Teddy gets fully involved in the mystery as it unfolds, and as the locked room murder is to Anty Boisjoly the clever caper is to Teddy Quillfeather. Smooth swindles and highwire heists, sticky fingers and weighted dice are grist for her mill. Clearly, she needs her own series to manage it all.

I hope you'll keep in touch for the imminent release of the first Teddy Quillfeather Mystery, more about which below…

There's a newsletter!

Anty Boisjoly minds the locked room murders while Teddy Quillfeather, now in her own series, handles heists and vice and counterfeit ice, and to help keep track of it all, plus cryptic clues and custom content and cartoons confined to the club, you can sign up for the combined Boisjoly/Quillfeather Infrequent Newsletter...
http://indefensiblepublishing.com/newsletters/

Anty Boisjoly Mysteries

The Case of the Canterfell Codicil
The first Anty Boisjoly mystery
In *The Case of the Canterfell Codicil,* Wodehousian gadabout and clubman Anty Boisjoly takes on his first case when his old Oxford chum and coxswain is facing the gallows, accused of the murder of his wealthy uncle. Not one but two locked-room mysteries later, Anty's matching wits and witticisms with a subversive butler, a senile footman, a single-minded detective-inspector, an irascible goat, and the eccentric conventions of the pastoral Sussex countryside to untangle a multi-layered mystery of secret bequests, ancient writs, love triangles, revenge, and a teasing twist in the final paragraph.

The Case of the Ghost of Christmas Morning
The Christmas number
Anty Boisjoly visits Aunty Boisjoly, his reclusive aunt, at her cosy, sixteen-bedroom burrow in snowy Hertfordshire, for a quiet Christmas in dairy country. But even before he arrives, a local war hero has not only been murdered in a most improbable fashion, but hours later he's standing his old friends Christmas drinks at the local. The only clues are footprints in the snow, leading to the only possible culprit — Aunty Boisjoly.

The Tale of the Tenpenny Tontine
The dual duel dilemma
It's another mystifying, manor house murder for bon-vivant and problem-solver Anty Boisjoly, when his clubmate asks him to determine who died first after a duel is fought in a locked room. The untold riches of the Tenpenny Tontine are in the balance, but the stakes only get higher when Anty determines that, duel or not, this was a case of murder.

The Case of the Carnaby Castle Curse

The scary one

The ancient curse of Carnaby Castle has begun taking victims again — either that, or someone's very cleverly done away with the new young bride of the philandering family patriarch, and the chief suspect is none other than Carnaby, London's finest club steward.

Anty Boisjoly's wits and witticisms are tested to their frozen limit as he sifts the superstitions, suspicions, and age-old schisms of the mediaeval Peak District village of Hoy to sort out how it was done before the curse can claim Carnaby himself.

Reckoning at the Riviera Royale

We finally meet Anty's mum and how to be banque at baccarat

Anty finally has that awkward 'did you murder my father' conversation with his mother while finding himself in the ticklish position of defending her and an innocent elephant against charges of impossible murder.

If that's not enough, Anty's fallen for the daughter of the mysterious mother-daughter team of gamblers, there's a second impossible murder, and Anty has a very worrying idea who it is that's been cheating the casino.

The Case of the Case of Kilcladdich

Time trickles down on a timeless tipple

Anty Boisjoly travels to the sacred source waters of Glen Glennegie to help decide the fate of his favourite whisky, but an impossible locked room murder is only one of a multitude of mysteries that try Anty's wits and witticisms to their northern limit.

Time trickles down on the traditional tipple as Anty unravels family feuds, ruptured romance, shepherdless sheep, and a series of suspiciously surfacing secrets to sort out who killed whom and how and why and who might be next to die.

Foreboding Foretelling at Ficklehouse Felling

Anty's reddest-of-herringed, twistiest-of-turned, locked-roomiest manor house mystery yet.

It's a classic, manor house, mystery-within-a-locked-room-mystery for Anty Boisjoly, when a death is foretold by a mystic that Anty's sure is a charlatan. But when an impossible murder follows the foretelling, Anty and his old ally and nemesis Inspector Wittersham must sift the connivance, contrivance, misguidance, and reliance on pseudoscience of the mad manor and its oddball inhabitants before the killer strikes again.

Mystery and Malice Aboard RMS Ballast

This one!

Anty, Vickers, Inspector Wittersham, and a passenger list of howling eccentrics find themselves prey to the sway and spray of the Scilly Seas when what at first seems a simple, unexplainable, locked-state-room murder twists into a tale of buried treasure, perilous weather and dangerous endeavours at sea.

Death Reports to a Health Resort

The next one!

We meet more of Anty's eccentric extended family when he visits his uncle at a retreat for fans of the first deadly sin and enthusiasts of the sixth. Motivated suspects are plump and plentiful when the most disliked man in the spa is the victim of a locked room murder, but Inspector Wittersham soon points the finger at Anty's uncle and things only get worse when a second murder occurs that both eye-witnesses — Anty Boisjoly and Ivor Wittersham — swear was impossible.

Made in United States
Troutdale, OR
03/27/2024

18736432R00128